"Try The Christmas Act On A Cowboy Who's Buying It,"

Jonah said. "You think you can sweep a lonely man off his feet by feeding him and kissing him and… Well, lady," he added flatly, "you've picked the wrong man. I'm not in the mood for a sweetheart, so you'll just have to contain your hugging urges until you find someone more accommodating. Unless the next time you grab me, you mean business."

"You insufferable—" Harmony's hands curled into fists at her sides, and the Christmas bells attached to them tinkled.

"Ho, ho, ho," Jonah said and slipped quietly out her bedroom door.

GW00372818

Dear Reader:

Welcome to Silhouette Desire®—provocative, compelling, contemporary love stories written by and for today's woman. These are stories to treasure.

Each and every Silhouette Desire is a wonderful romance in which the emotional and the sensual go hand in hand. When you open a Desire™, you enter a whole new world—a world that has, naturally, a perfect hero just waiting to whisk you away! A Silhouette Desire can be light-hearted or serious, but it will always be satisfying.

We hope you enjoy this Desire today—and will go on to enjoy many more.

Please write to us:

Jane Nicholls
Silhouette Books
PO Box 236
Thornton Road
Croydon
Surrey
CR9 3RU

Miracles and Mistletoe

CAIT LONDON

™ SILHOUETTE

Desire ®

All the characters in this book have no existence outside the imagination of the author, and have no relation whatsoever to anyone bearing the same name or names. They are not even distantly inspired by any individual known or unknown to the author, and all the incidents are pure invention.

*First published in Great Britain 1996
Silhouette Books, Eton House, 18-24 Paradise Road,
Richmond, Surrey TW9 1SR*

© Lois Kleinsasser 1995

ISBN 0 373 05968 X

22-9612

*Printed and bound in Great Britain
by Mackays of Chatham PLC, Chatham*

CAIT LONDON

lives in the Missouri Ozarks, but loves to travel the Northwest's gold-rush/cattle-drive trails every summer. She loves research trips, meeting people and going to Native American dances. Ms London is an avid reader who loves to paint, play with computers and grow herbs (particularly scented geraniums). She's a national bestselling and award-winning author and she also writes historical romances under another pseudonym. Three is her lucky number; she has three daughters, and the events in her life have always been in threes. "I love writing for Silhouette," she says. "One of the best perks about all this hard work is the thrilling reader response and the warm, snug sense that I have given readers an enjoyable, entertaining gift."

One

"Sweetheart, I don't like talking to you any better than you like my company," Jonah said to his dog. He spoke aloud, though he had been mentally conversing with her. "And no, I'm not exactly wallowing in Christmas cheer."

Shrimp—the runt of the litter and now a four-year-old female collie—regally eyed him from her side of the pickup. Earlier in the cold December day, Shrimp had balked when Jonah had called her. He knew she preferred to be called Sylvia or anything elegant and feminine.

Had she balked because she resented her name? Or was it the desperation in his tone?

Jonah's glove-clad hands tightened on the steering wheel of his battered pickup. Two weeks before Christmas found him chatting mentally with his dog. January might find him talking with his small herd of cattle or a passing bird, he realized grimly; they would all have a gay old time while he lost whatever sanity he now possessed.

He glanced at the snow-covered wheat fields surrounding Fort Benton, a small historic community in rural Montana. The snowfall had threatened for days and now promised to become a blizzard, wrapped in thirty below zero weather.

Shrimp continued to stare at him and Jonah said grimly, "Yes, sweetheart, I just might take June Fields up on her offer."

He glared at the collie and stated flatly, "Of course I know sex isn't love. And no, I'm not like some old Montana lone wolf howling at the moon."

Jonah decided to ignore Shrimp's righteous, condemning brown-eyed stare. When a man feared losing his mind, he took drastic action. June Fields, an amorous triple-divorced woman, represented the depth of Jonah's desperation. She'd been flirting with him since his wife died thirteen years ago, and Jonah would try anything to stop the sliding of his mind—only he could hear the child crying....

"'Meaningless sex?' Don't think you're a notch above me, Shrimp. You've been mooning over that statue of Shep since the town put it up. Magnificent? He's only a bronze likeness of a dog that died in 1942. At least I'm after a live body," he muttered. "So we're both nuts. And I am just desperate enough to spend the night in June's bed. I'd do anything to have a full night's sleep—or even a few hours."

He glanced at his dog's accusing stare and cursed. "Yes, sweetheart. Even sex with a woman who has been after me for years and has married twice between. And no, I don't think I'll be permanently injured. People have survived sex after forty."

Jonah closed his eyes momentarily, then stated grimly, "Okay. You're right. I am forty-five, not forty. And don't tell me to have a Merry Christmas. Nothing good lasts, and Christmas cheer is for other people."

The narrow winding highway before him demanded all his attention. In constant repair, the road would take him past small alkali lakes and down into Fort Benton. Laden with blocks of concrete, his battered pickup passed over the four inches of new snow. A sudden gust of wind pushed at it and Jonah held his breath, controlling the vehicle around another winding curve.

The child's sobs haunted his waking hours now. The sounds lurked around him, quivering sadly on the harsh, howling winter wind.

Jonah swallowed the emotion tightening his throat.

He'd heard a child cry like that once—his daughter, Grace, crying for a dying newborn calf. Now Grace was lying beside her mother in the local cemetery. Maggie and he had waited eight long years for Grace. . . .

Jonah glanced at the frozen alkali lakes where buffalo used to wallow. Grace would have been thirteen now, laughing at life and filled with an eagerness to meet it. Jonah would be facing her questions about boys and romance; he'd secretly studied about the changes a girl makes when she becomes a woman and try his best to understand her needs.

Another gust of wind thrust at his pickup and Jonah tumbled back into the past. Five years ago, on a late-winter afternoon just like this one—gray, freezing and windy—he'd been taking Grace to a Christmas party. The doll she had wanted so badly had been wrapped and hidden in the seat behind him. His pickup, shiny and new back then, had slid off the road and Jonah had fought to control it.

The pickup had tilted into a snowdrift, but they were safe and uninjured. *Jonah had to get help; he had to take his daughter to warmth.*

He glanced at the left front fender and the dent that had happened that night. The snow had begun falling heavily in the thirty-below-zero weather, the windchill lowering.

He had to leave his daughter alone. She was just eight—a laughing, loving child—she wouldn't have survived out in the fierce, freezing temperatures. Grace had promised to stay bundled in the protection and blankets of the pickup's cab while he tried to flag help.

Jonah had struggled up the incline to the highway and waited, freezing and praying for help. He'd returned to the pickup five times to find Grace safe. She had promised each time to stay huddled in the blankets and not leave the pickup.

The sixth trip back to check on her, Jonah had found the pickup door wide open, banging in the wind. Grace was gone.

They said he went crazy that day, hunting for her in the blizzard.

They said that his wife's death in childbirth had torn his heart deeply; they worried that Jonah would die without his daughter.

When they found her, Grace looked as if she were sleeping, holding the puppy she had left the pickup to rescue.

Now Jonah fought the desperate pain and guilt washing over him. The Bear Paw Mountains and Square Butte stood in the distance just as they had then, ancient landmarks.

Grace had never gotten his Christmas present, the doll she'd wanted so much.

Deep in his thoughts, Jonah glanced at the moving van, tilting off at an angle from the highway. Only a fool would drive tires with little tread in the winter. From the look of the deep snowdrift around it, the driver had already caught a ride into town.

If only the crying would stop.... Jonah fought to control his thoughts, forcing them away from the slanting, perilous abyss that scared the hell out of him.

He'd gone off the deep end a long time ago. He'd mourned and cursed and drank. Then he'd pulled himself together and settled in for a lonely life. Crop failures and falling cattle market prices hadn't really mattered. By working for others, he'd kept the land his great-great-grandfather had homesteaded. Cy Fargo had left a heritage of Western endurance and brilliant blue eyes. Jonah's Blackfoot great-great-grandmother had given the Fargos raven hair, dark skin and the rumor that she'd had certain powers.

Jonah ran his glove along his jaw and realized that nothing had reached into him until six months ago.

When the child began to cry.... The sobs reached into his heart, tearing it apart.

"Yes, I see him," Jonah said to Shrimp as he eased his pickup to a stop. His head was throbbing painfully now. Maybe that was the sign of a man's last sane moments. "Only a fool would try to drive a rig like that in weather like this."

Walking along the side of the road, the "fool" waved gaily. A curtain of snow shielded the figure running to him. Jonah sat in his pickup and waited. All he needed was some cowboy dumb enough to be out—

A woman's cheery grin appeared at his window.

Jonah stared back at her. A fool *woman,* he corrected. She had "city" written all over her pale, happy face. A female stranger who didn't know that Montana blizzards could kill ... or that she could be smiling at a possible Montana strangler.

She rapped on his window, forcing him to roll it down. "Yes, get in," Jonah said grimly. "You can ride into town with me. You'll have to come back for your rig tomorrow. It's too cold and too late to deal with that now."

While the woman hurried around the front of his pickup, Jonah ordered Shrimp to scoot next to him. Shrimp refused and Jonah realized again that he had not spoken aloud to his dog. His mind was truly tilting— He chewed on that discomforting tidbit while the woman opened the passenger side of the pickup and looked hopefully at him. Shrimp hopped out of the pickup and waited. Jonah sighed. "The dog likes the window side. You'll have to sit in the middle."

"Great! This is so nice of you. I really, really appreciate this. I was getting a bit cold." The woman climbed in beside him, bringing with her feminine scents, a happy holiday air and the tinkling of tiny bells. She licked a snowflake from her bottom lip with the tip of her tongue.

Jonah edged away from her body as she settled close to him. He tapped his fingers on the steering wheel, and when she was finished adjusting herself, he set the pickup in gear.

He glanced down at her warm knitted scarf, decorated with holly, and flicked it from his sleeve.

He tensed, sensing the elements of the woman—caring, cuddling, strength...storms, lightning and melting heat. Then he imagined a sweet spring wind riffling a calm lake and woodland flowers ... He sensed walls and pain, and closed his eyes against the wash of impressions. He closed whatever was going on in his mind, uncomfortable with his thoughts. She was no more than a woman who didn't know enough to stay put in dangerous weather.

His intruder swept off her knitted cap and gloves. Clear honey-brown eyes framed by bristling dark brown lashes smiled up at him. Her hair, a light coppery mass of long, spiraling curls, seemed to bounce with excitement and happiness. Jonah closed his eyes and wondered why the only passerby had to be himself; he wasn't in the mood for contagious Christmas cheer.

The woman reeked of Christmas; she was saturated in it from her jumbled curls down to her uptown, neon-pink snow boots. He eased down into his coat, hoping to discourage her from chitchat.

She pushed away a gleaming tendril from her cheek and nodded to the ditch. "That's my moving truck back there. I waited for an hour after going off the road, then left it. That's what they say to do, isn't it? Stay in the protection of the vehicle until someone comes along? But I was just so excited about moving here. I'll be sharing Christmas with my brother's family. Imagine— Christmas morning and children exclaiming over their Santa Claus stocking goodies. I hope they get up early, so I can dig into my own stocking."

Her tone was breathless and filled with excitement. Her pink lips curved with joyous expectation. She unbuttoned her bright yellow down coat and her body wiggled briefly, settling too close to him. Jonah grimly moved his worn shearling coat sleeve away from hers.

"Uh-huh," Jonah muttered, concentrating on the road and hoping that his don't-talk warning tone would stop her motor mouth. Here he was, concentrating on snow-covered roads, trapped with a grown woman—somewhere in her mid-thirties—who was excited about her Santa Claus stocking. The snow was falling heavily now. Just as heavily as that day five years ago—

"My name is Harmony Davis." His intruder's cheerful feminine voice ripped him back from the perilous edge where the child's sobs lurked. Harmony chafed elegant, slender hands together and blew on them for warmth; Jonah turned up the heater a notch. While he preferred cold, he didn't want to be responsible for her becoming ill. Her shoulder bumped his arm as she shivered and he eased stiffly away.

"You may know my brother, Pax," she said. "He and his wife just moved here three years ago. They bought the old Sayers place. I've only seen the children on their brief visits to Des Moines. I can't wait until Christmas, when his children open their presents from me. I love giving gifts more than opening them myself."

He noted the bright gold sweater beneath her coat. Her clothing was expensive and new.

He noted her breasts and inhaled sharply. He frowned at the surge of raw hunger gripping his body. Harmony frowned slightly as if something disturbed her, then she continued in that happy, excited tone, "Pax loves it here. That's why I decided to move closer to my brother. I adore his three little urchins, and with Christmas coming, I wanted us all to be together. Then I thought, 'What about Valentine's Day? And Easter?' So I decided to move near them, just like that."

She moved restlessly, nestling close to him as if she were his best girl out on a Sunday drive. Jonah didn't want her Christmas cheer or best girls or attachments of the heart; he couldn't take a third round of pain.

Jonah's heart clenched painfully. Each year, he dreaded the holiday season and he promised for the hundredth time that he would not be "hunkering" on the outskirts of someone else's family on Christmas Eve.

"Uh-huh." He didn't want her cheerful, excited tone intruding upon his dark thoughts. She had the look and the sound of a do-gooder and he'd had a bellyful of them when his wife died suddenly and when Grace—

He also didn't like the vision of her face that remained with him, though he was staring at the snow-covered highway. The color of her eyes had jarred him—tawny, the shade of old gold, with dark flecks in their depths. He'd glimpsed the angular set of her jaw, softened by that jumbled mass of shiny light red gold curls and an expressive mouth meant for kissing.

That mouth was mobile, soft and glossy pink, and reminded him of a rosebud about to flower.

While she shared Pax's tawny shades, he was darker with a wild, fierce angular look that settled well into Montana. Pax could be imposing—a man filled with pride, love for his family and an obstinate talent for trying to be Jonah's friend. Harmony's face was striking, not pretty or classic, and the summer sun might sprinkle tiny freckles and honey-gold on her skin. Harmony was a bold, Celtic-looking woman, and one who apparently didn't know when welcome doors had slammed shut in her face.

Jonah thought he heard Shrimp snickering about his "kissing" thought. He stealthily blew away a clinging curl from his shoulder and glanced at Shrimp. From the passenger side of the pickup, the dog looked at him innocently.

"What's your name?" the woman asked in a tone that was warm and husky as she draped her arm around Shrimp. She hugged the dog and the tiny gold bells on her bracelet jingled merrily. "You're beautiful," she told the dog, nuzzling Shrimp's warm fur.

Shrimp smirked at Jonah and the woman looked at Jonah and repeated, "Your name?"

"Fargo. Jonah Fargo. That's Shrimp." He disliked being sucked into holiday-cheer chitchat.

Harmony turned to him, her amber-shaded eyes wide and warm. The dim light caught the thin gold hoops in her ears. "Oh, I'm so glad to meet you. Pax said you helped him harvest his wheat crops and taught him about raising cows. He thinks highly of you."

Because everything was chipper in her world and nothing was going well in his life, Jonah resented her intrusion. He resented the slight bumping of her body against his, the woman scents swirling around his pickup. "Cattle," he corrected grimly. "Not cows... cattle."

He ignored her bright grin up at him. He sank his jaw deeper in his turned-up coat collar and hoped that the woman would take his hint and be quiet. The long spiraling curl resting on his shoulder glistened, nudging his dark mood. He shrugged gently and the curl was joined by others. He forced his attention to the road.

"You like quiet, don't you?" Harmony asked, peering out into heavy snowfall and the dying light.

Jonah didn't respond. Pax had said he had a sister in Iowa; he didn't say how much she talked. Her fresh spring scents and an elusive, exotic musk invaded Jonah's privacy. He preferred leather and smoke and animal scents. He could trust them just as he trusted the sense of solitude that she was also invading.

"I will see that you're repaid for this kindness. But please, I don't want to take you out of your way," Harmony was saying.

Jonah inhaled. On his way to where? Where was his life going? Six more months of listening to the child cry would be unbearable. "You won't take me out of my way. I'm headed right past Pax's place on my way to town."

Harmony frowned slightly and peered into the snow flurries. "Pax said your place was next to his. We must be miles from there in the opposite direction of town. Or maybe I've made a mistake while reading my map. I didn't have any problem on the interstate, but these back roads—"

"Could be." Jonah had begun the day just driving in the opposite direction from town—going anyplace to escape his house, where a dish had just inexplicably lifted from the table and smashed against the wall. He cursed mentally; Shrimp looked dismayed, as if her master was making a poor first impression and embarrassing her. Harmony straightened in her seat.

He'd decided to take June up on her long-time offer and had turned back toward town in the early afternoon.

Shrimp eyed him with a tsk-tsk expression and Jonah scowled back. Sex with June was the only thing he hadn't tried to stop the sounds in his head.

"... I'm finally here. All this history—fur traders, outlaws and steamboats on the upper Missouri River. And I'm here just in time for Christmas," Harmony said with excitement lacing her husky tone. "I can almost see the buffalo roaming the prairie—"

Harmony turned to him too quickly and Jonah realized he'd been gritting his teeth. He also realized that his gaze had been taking in the lush curves in Harmony's gold sweater. A tiny cupid suspended from a gold chain glittered each time she inhaled.

She eased away slightly and stared at the road; her "isn't-Christmas-great?" excitement slipped a bit.

Jonah closed his lids briefly to erase the sight of her breasts. He shifted into a lower gear, easing the pickup around a wide curve. Harmony's long, pale fingers gripped her jeans-clad thighs and Jonah wondered how they would feel digging into his back while—

He desperately wanted those soft full breasts pressed against his bare chest. Just bodies against each other, nothing between them but hunger and the momentary relief of his tormented mind. From the look of his woman passenger, she'd need a strong man to keep her happy.

Harmony turned quickly to frown at him and Shrimp whined as if begging him not to make a poor showing. A slow blush began moving up Harmony's cheeks and the gleaming hoops in her ears trembled. The bells on her bracelet jingled when she reached to smooth her spiraling curls. "I hope you have a nice Christmas, too," she murmured in a very polite tone.

Jonah wondered if her curls would feel like silk as they wrapped around his fingers. Or spilled across his chest. He'd like to bury his face in her scents and forget that he was losing his mind.

Harmony inhaled as if pricked by a pin and Jonah's whole body tensed, shocking him. At forty-five, he knew his body well; every muscle ached with sensual need, and he could almost feel the steam rise from him to fog the window.

"Pax thinks that the old cabin at the edge of his property will be just perfect for me," Harmony stated, her cheery tone sliding into one of caution.

Jonah wondered how that husky voice would sound while they were making love—

Harmony looked at him sharply and Shrimp turned slowly to look at the snow outside the window. His collie didn't want to be associated with him just now.

Harmony shifted restlessly and Jonah's unwilling glance followed her long legs down to heavy winter boots. She cleared her throat. "Ah...is this an unusually cold winter? I mean the temperature is thirty below zero and the windchill is much lower than that."

"What the hell were you doing out in it?" Jonah asked sharply, irritated by her scents and his uncertain mood. "Why aren't you home with your husband and children?"

Her brows arched as she looked at him and Jonah sensed a flash of steel beneath her femininity. "What were *you* doing out in it? And I don't have a husband or children."

"I have a right to be here. *I* live here," he stated in a tone as if explaining a fact to a child.

She smiled tightly, quickly, not giving an inch. "*I'm* moving here."

"Harmony," he said, tasting the name grimly and marking it in his mental black book of people to avoid. It belonged in a fairy tale, and to Jonah, life was not flowers and elves. Life was pain and *the sound of the child crying*.

He tried to think of June's curves against him, undulating beneath him, taking him to a momentary physical explosion and then peace. Just a few more miles and he could drop his unwelcome-Christmas-cheer lady at Pax's ranch, then he could go to June. She'd be surprised, but she'd welcome him. They'd probably have a drink and then ... or she might just reach for him. He hoped she would reach for him because he didn't want talking tonight. June would know what he wanted and know that he didn't want commitments. She was that kind of lady. He resented the scents filling his pickup and tangling his senses and he resented the woman beside him. "You should have picked a better time to move."

She was blushing and glaring at him. She was bristling with tempered anger. "You're a widower," she said in a low, hushed tone. "And a lonely man at Christmas time. I understand how a night like this would make you want company."

"No need to understand anything, lady," Jonah shot back. Pax must have told her about Jonah's past. The pickup slid to the edge of the road and he eased it back into the center.

Harmony leaned forward, ignoring him as she peered into the darkness. "The snow is worse. Please don't go out of your way to take me to Pax's. I can stay at the first place we come to. I'll call him from there."

"Uh-huh," Jonah agreed without enthusiasm. The first place was his ranch and she wasn't staying there. He'd get her to Pax's if he had to pull the pickup through the snow like Humphrey Bogart pulled the *African Queen* boat down the swamp. Unless Santa and his flying reindeer would take her off Jonah's hands.

They drove in silence, snowflakes hurling at the windshield. Then Harmony said quietly, precisely, "Your aura is very dark, Jonah. Ending your life on a night like this won't help. Neither will an athletic woman and sexual medication."

"'Aura ... sexual medication,'" he repeated. "Are you my mother?" he demanded roughly, shaken that she had exposed a thought he had buried from himself. Hidden beneath layers of control, Jonah had wondered if he should have died with his daughter.

When he suddenly realized he'd said nothing about June and his needs, he glanced at her sharply. "What made you say that about an 'athletic woman and sexual medication'? And what do you know about my aura?"

"I just know." Her amber eyes were very soft, overpowering the pale contours of her face and glowing in the light of the dashboard. "I know you're hurting and striking out at what you don't understand. Why don't you try focusing on Christmas?"

"Leave it," Jonah ordered harshly. He'd had enough of do-gooders to last him until forever.

Harmony inhaled sharply. Jonah Fargo was tough, scarred and rude. His aura was that of a wounded lone timber wolf, striking out at his pain.

She shifted abruptly, startled by the sense of heat and need swirling from him. She eased her leg away from his hand as he shifted into a lower gear. This cowboy's hands were big and could possess what he wanted—

Jonah Fargo wanted a woman; he wanted the red-hot desire to empty his mind, the physical strain to ease his tension so that he could sleep—even for a short time. This Jonah Fargo was walking a tight line and feared falling into darkness....

Harmony shivered slightly despite the warmth of the pickup. The tall, lean Westerner resented her presence, and frankly she wasn't exactly happy with him, though he had probably saved her life. Between his worn Western hat and his turned-up shearling collar, she noted his weathered skin covered by the day's growth of dark stubble. His mouth was grim, bracketed by lines of pain.

She wanted to touch soothe those harsh lines, to heal them. She placed her hand over the bells on her other wrist. They reminded her not to reach out too quickly, to act as her heart dictated. She had been very careful to listen to her warning alarms and to focus her life away from her powers.

Harmony studied her long, pale tapering fingers. She did have the power to heal, but she had learned to suppress it. She could take the pain of others into herself, relieving them, and healing. If the wounds were deep, the danger to herself was strong. She also could read thoughts. What she was, who she was had frightened Mark so much that he couldn't bear to be near her—unless she would help him in high-stakes gambling. She'd refused to use her abilities to his advantage; Mark had been outraged and had struck her for the first and last time. "A freak," he had called her before their divorce. "I'm glad we didn't have kids.... They might have been freaks like you."

At twenty-five she'd been shattered. Now at thirty-nine, she had come to terms with who and what she was—a top-rate coppersmith, who did not allow her impulses or her powers to rule her.

She glanced at the frozen countryside and knew that the cheery holiday season always tossed unhappy memories at her. At twenty-six, she had barely survived, licking her wounds after her marriage failed. Then she'd stopped by a terrible auto accident and worked desperately—using her powers, straining to make a small boy and his mother live. The small town had been cruel and disbelieving in her psychic powers, her ability to heal. Then she'd moved to Des Moines and had wrapped the city around her. She'd learned to be very cautious, healing quietly, unobtrusively when she could.

She'd learned to shield her impulses and to forget Mark.

Now, if a nice, easygoing, intellectual man crossed her path, one who understood the possibility of psychic phenomena and one whose company she enjoyed—a companionable, soothing man—she might be receptive. With like interests, gentle conversation and his acceptance of what she was...Harmony might consider an arrangement. A balanced, smooth-flowing relationship with lots of space on both sides. A balanced, mutual, scheduled interaction between friends who respected each other.

Sex. The image ripped across her mind, laying a scene of a man and a woman desperately tangled together. Realizing instantly that Jonah's thoughts had leapt into her mind, she refused to look at him. Hunger and the desire smashed at her in hot, tight waves.

Though she had tasted desire with her ex-husband, Harmony was stunned by the vision and the mating.

Mating. Bonding. Two hearts becoming one, melded by the white-hot fires of desire. Then there was the softness, the soothing of hearts and bodies, the sweetness... She saw Jonah's hard expression ease, his blue eyes soften with tenderness. The woman's face was shadowed, her body pale and soft against his dark, hard length. Though their moment had passed, Jonah kept the woman close to him, protecting her, soothing her. He was caressing her then, a lover's touch. There were old-fashioned Western phrases spoken in a deep, tender tone. Gold flashed as the woman removed her necklace to place it around his neck. Then the boyish, sweet Jonah was teasing his best girl and beginning to love her all over again....

Harmony swallowed tightly and blinked away the image. She had never known sex could be that heated, nor that tender. She realized now that she had never bonded, never truly mated with her ex-husband. Not like Jonah and the woman in his arms. They had tested the softness, the steel of each other, pushing, caressing, needing, sharing, giving.... The ancient dance of a man and a woman was a ceremony, a marriage and a bonding forged by becoming one body, one heart, one mind....

Mark had taken— Harmony inhaled sharply, refusing to review her failed marriage. She glanced at Jonah, who was concentrating on the road. The man's desperation wrapped around her and she attempted a reading, probing his thoughts. Perhaps the woman in his arms had been his wife... perhaps the woman he sought, June.

Harmony's fingers tightened on her crossed arms. She had feared releasing her desire for Mark. Or did she have intense passions for him? She tossed the thought away; long ago, she had realized that her powers prevented her from releasing the depths of her desire. Long ago, she had dismissed the notion that she could bond with the other half of her heart—a man who could understand and not fear her.... The relationship wouldn't be playful or teasing or especially dramatic, à la grand passion, but comfortable and gentle.

From the shadows of his Western hat, Jonah's startling blue eyes shot down at her. "Did you say something?"

Shrimp barked lightly and licked Harmony's cheek as if apologizing for her master's poor manners. Harmony sensed the collie's love and concern for Jonah.

And Shrimp's longing for Shep.

"I asked, 'Who's Shep?'" Harmony said, then added cautiously, "Pax said something about him."

"A sheepherder's faithful dog. The town placed a statue of him on the Missouri riverfront." Jonah rubbed his temple impatiently.

"Do you have a headache?" Harmony knew he would resist her touch, the ease she could give him if only for a short time.

"Now I do," he said roughly. "I like quiet."

While Harmony liked solitude and quiet, too, she also liked gentle, considerate men with polite manners. "And a Merry Christmas to you, too," she muttered as Shrimp licked her cheek again and moved closer as if to console her.

Jonah glared at Shrimp. "*You* behave," he said as if returning an order.

To shield her grin, Harmony lowered her chin into her collar. Unless she was mistaken, the collie had just put her paw down on Jonah's poor manners.

"I make cupids," she offered cheerily, sliding her happy little cherubs into Jonah's ominous mood. He wasn't darkening her Christmas cheer. He was already angry; she might as well toss her cupids where she wanted. Harmony pictured the chubby cherubs fluttering around the tough cowboy's black hat and tumbling on the worn denim covering his thigh. The scene consoled her taut nerves.

Harmony was used to people flowing easily through her life, and Jonah was like the huge black rock landmark she had passed before the wreck—immovable and shrouded in gloom.

To avenge his interference with her excitement and his lack of Christmas cheer, she threw another mental cupid at his hat.

Jonah brushed his leather glove through the air by his hat as if disturbed by an insect. He briskly rubbed his thigh, where Harmony had pictured cupids playing. "Cupids," Harmony repeated, smiling. "I'm a coppersmith really, but I work in other metals like tin. The market now is great for cupids. I can work anywhere and ship them to buyers. That's why staying close to Pax is so great—"

"Lady, I am trying to keep us on the road. Would you mind shutting the hell up?" Jonah asked tightly.

Sex with June won't help. Harmony crossed her arms over her chest and settled back with her thoughts. She wasn't any happier than Jonah was, her mood unfamiliar and unwelcome. She probed Jonah's mind and stopped abruptly. He was bitter and frustrated and cursing his poor luck to have a "dingbat heifer" dropped on him by fate. Shrimp's Jonah was a chatty cowboy after all, though no one would know it.

A curtain slowly, firmly, lowered and Jonah's thoughts were sealed from her.

Harmony tensed. The cowboy had powers; they weren't strong, but they were emerging. "Reading" him—concentrating on his emotions, his thoughts—and translating them would be impossible if he decided to block her. His abilities hovered on the edge; he had inherited them, just as she and her brother, Pax, had received theirs. Jonah's powers had come from an ancient line, too.

Jonah Fargo had undeveloped abilities to act as a sender or a reader. He had blocked his talents with disbelief in the paranormal.

A flame lashed at her—within it a man and woman, pulsed deep in the act of lovemaking. Jonah's driving need for sex leapt at her, shocking her. Not a loving tender relationship, but mind-blanking, hot sex with a woman he had put off for years. She was a last effort to grip reality. He should feel guilty about using poor June—

"You're irritating me," he said aloud in a low, dangerous tone. "Whatever you're doing to get my attention, stop it."

"Stop! Let me out. I refuse to ride with you, no matter how cold it is or how deep the snow is," Harmony ordered instantly, her anger rising in a flash fire. She shot out a hand to grip the door lever. She trembled, realizing that no one, not even Mark, had caused her to react so sharply.

Mark had hurt her deepest, most private feminine soul. If Jonah Fargo had one good point, it was that she didn't sense she needed to hold back her anger or her emotions with him. She wanted to rip into him without her usual sensitivity, she wanted to bare her anger and confront the arrogant, impolite—

She met Jonah's thunderous dark blue gaze. "You are rude, cowboy."

"So what?" he asked uncaringly, and began to ease the pickup off the road. They passed between two posts supporting a huge metal sign. "That says Fargo. This is my ranch. There's no way I can take you to Pax's place tonight. You'll have to stay at my place until he can come get you. You can call him and talk all you want to him," he said in a defeated, gloomy tone. "I'd just appreciate it if you didn't talk me to death."

Shrimp whined and looked at Harmony with big, liquidy brown eyes, as if begging for her company.

From the shadows of his hat, Jonah eyed the two females looking back at him. Then he groaned mentally, longing for June's warm bed. The thought rasped across Harmony's taut nerves.

"If you think I'm happy about the arrangements, you are very much mistaken, mister," Harmony stated tightly.

Two

When the door to Jonah's small house swung open two hours later, Harmony was just sampling her beef-and-barley stew. Earlier, Jonah had pointed her toward the house and mumbled that he had to take care of the stock in the barn. She doubted horses and cows were the reason he hadn't returned sooner.

The house was littered with magazines, shelves of Native American artifacts and petrified prehistoric shells. Dinosaur teeth, huge rocklike objects, were obviously treasured, placed in an exact row over magazines on Jonah's coffee table.

Jonah entered the kitchen in a flurry of snowflakes, his longish hair whipping around his face. The bald ceiling light caught the strong features of his face as his blue eyes swung to her. His gaze pierced her accusingly for invading his domain— an empty house with battered furniture and lighter squares on his paneled walls where pictures once hung. A saddle was propped where a Christmas tree should have been, and he'd clearly been sleeping on the sagging couch when there were beautiful, antique wrought-iron beds in the three rooms.

Harmony had made the beds and turned the blankets down to catch the heat. The beds were soft and welcoming, though lack of sleep lay stamped on Jonah's harsh features.

No one had softened Jonah's hard life and he mourned his wife and daughter.

The healing need within Harmony cried out to touch him. To soothe that fierce expression of pain. In the unforgiving light, Jonah's rugged face was shadowed, circles haunting his unusual sky-blue eyes. The black stubble covering his hard jaw shifted, as though he were gritting his teeth. He bore his black mood and his pain like a cape, swirling around him. He was not Mr. Merry Christmas.

She gripped the bells at her wrist, steeling herself against reaching out to him.

His gaze ripped down her body and the raw surge of his needs thrust against Harmony. She shivered and straightened and faced him, her fingers releasing the bells. She no longer wanted to reach out to him; she wanted to protect herself—to keep her life running smoothly, and she sensed that Jonah was a danger to her.

"You look like a warlord home from the range," Harmony said lightly, not allowing her emotions to escape. This man troubled her deeply; he challenged her on a deep, primitive level, and she sensed that he could change her life forever.

Fierce, sexually hungry, hot-tempered, lone-wolf warriors battling their talents were not on her Christmas menu du jour. His aura was swift, action packed and decisive, slicing at softness not necessary to him.

Jonah Fargo was a man at the end of his proverbial rope. He tore off his gloves, then he slapped them into his hat before sailing it to the washer. His dark fingers flipped open the buttons of his battered shearling coat; he discarded it on a huge rocking chair by the stove. He stood very still, his head lifted at an angle, and she sensed him testing the scents of the room, prowling through them. To a man living alone for years, the scents and sounds were unfamiliar and disturbing.

A man who moved quickly, purposefully, Jonah Fargo possessed a lithe grace that was frightening in his anger.

He glanced at the washer, which Harmony had filled with his dirty clothing. Rage trembled around him, pain shot through

him like lightning bolts. Jonah Fargo stood there, a glowering
warlord of a man, long legs locked at the knee, spoiling for a
fight.

He didn't like sharing his lair with her, the Christmas-reeking
invader.

Shrimp leapt to her feet and stood in front of Harmony.
Jonah's lips tightened, his eyes glancing at his dog, then back
to Harmony.

She refused to rise to anger, to rise to Jonah's stormy mood.
After all, it was the holiday season when people should be filled
with goodwill. She hadn't lost her temper—ever—and she
didn't intend to have her Christmas cheer trampled by the snow-
covered Western boots of Jonah Fargo.

Harmony disliked confrontation; she liked her life's cogs re-
volving smoothly. She always avoided people like the tough
cowboy, the ones with raw edges and maddening manners.

She shrugged mentally; the Christmas season was for loving
and warmth. Jonah would just have to lump her happiness. She
plunged the wooden spoon into the pot bubbling on the old
stove and lifted the aromatic stew toward Jonah, offering him
a sample. "Would you like a taste?"

"What have you done, woman?" Jonah demanded in a
harsh, deep voice as he looked slowly around his small home.

*Woman. Antiquated dominant, arrogant warrior male term
used for the female species. Generic term for the species not
male, and having surface fat contained in curves.*

"I merely cooked supper with the few groceries I could
find," she returned too quickly, too sharply, and immediately
regretted rising mentally to Jonah's thrust. Jonah's home was
worn and barren, just like his stove and refrigerator. To a
woman used to cooking, with window-sill-potted herbs waiting for her, Jonah's empty cupboards presented a challenge.
The frozen steak would serve two people now, simmering in a
tasteful mix of carrots, onion and barley. He should darn well
appreciate a hot, nourishing meal in a blizzard.

He kicked aside a pile of separated laundry waiting on the
linoleum floor and walked around the perimeter of the living
room, glancing into the opened doors of the three bedrooms.
He slammed each bedroom door and the bathroom door,
which promptly slanted, one hinge coming away from the

doorframe. "Keep these shut. Keeps the heat in the living room," he ordered, sprawling into the old rocker and looking at the gas heating stove as if the flames could tell him how to extract Harmony from his premises.

The winter wind howled around the house; Harmony's uncertain temper nudged her control as she ladled the stew into bowls and placed the biscuits she had baked on the table. She liked cooking and family dinners, but with Jonah gnawing on his temper—

He glanced at her, his eyes a startling shade of blue against his dark skin, new beard and black hair. She noted the softening wave at the nape of his neck and the tense muscles of his jaw and throat.

Jonah's gaze changed, shielded by his lashes as he looked down her body. In the middle of placing the butter on the old wooden table, Harmony hesitated, shaken by Jonah's slow visual tasting of her hair, her shoulders, breasts and hips.

The male species studying the female, his ears pointing.

Her buttocks tightened as she caught the image of his large hands gripping her tightly, easing her against the thrust of him—

Harmony swallowed instantly, aware that her breasts had responded, suddenly sensitive. She blamed the cold; then Jonah's gaze locked to the cupid pendant resting between her breasts.

She slammed the butter plate onto the table. "Come eat," she said, in an unfamiliar sharp tone. She usually wore layers of loose, flowing clothes, or long, swirling skirts. However, the black jeans and the sweater had suited traveling and her western destination. With Jonah nearby, she regretted her choice.

There was nothing wrong with her jeans. Or her sweater. The freezing temperatures, her frightening slide into the ditch and meeting Jonah Fargo could nettle the calmest person.

She shivered, sensing an exploration of her body, a soft touch here, a smoothing one across her lower stomach, then a firm cupping of her femininity—

"Since you're stuck here, don't think you can take over," Jonah said. He walked to the table, loomed over her, and Harmony stepped back too quickly.

Jonah was too large, his mood too fierce, his aura too potently sexual now.

Six-feet-three inches of pure muscle and frustration, Jonah in a dark mood could terrify anyone, Harmony reasoned. She refused to be intimidated, tilting her head up to him. At five-foot-eight, she rarely felt small or very feminine.

Jonah's size—or was it his aura?—caused her to feel delicate and womanly...desirable...needed by a man.... The picture of Jonah and his playmate burning inside a flame scorched Harmony.

Unable to bear his swirling passions—anger, frustration, elemental desire—she slid quickly into her chair and was surprised to find Jonah acting the gentleman and easing her to the table. He sat slowly and looked at the bowls of steaming soup and the freshly baked biscuits. "Thanks," he said finally, as if a distant reminder had dragged good manners from him.

"You're welcome." The small sign that he had been gentled slightly was encouraging.

A storm of Jonah's memories went zipping by Harmony as he stirred the spoon and studied the rich broth. Another woman had cooked nourishing soup, a child's spoon had sought the pasta alphabet letters. G-R-A-C-E. The pain within him caused her to reach out to touch his dark hand with her fingers and the spoon stopped. Jonah lifted his haunted, rugged face and glared at her. "Don't ever touch me, lady," he said too quietly.

She'd wanted to ease him; she'd rarely reached out to others so impulsively. The need to heal, the ability, had proven very dangerous. She studied her trembling fingers, curling them protectively into her palms. Her nails bit into the slightly callused skin. When would she learn not to open herself, to give too quickly?

Harmony frowned, aware of Jonah circling her, though he hadn't moved. He was silent, watching her with a troubled frown.

"Are you afraid of me?" he asked roughly. "Of being alone...here with me?" Then he answered his question, his fingers slashing through the thick black hair, the gray at his temples glistening in the light. He ran his hand across his jaw, and the rough sound caused the hair on Harmony's nape to rise. "Look," he said slowly. "I'm a little rough around the edges right now. I guess I'll stay that way. The wreck probably didn't help your nerves. But you're safe and warm. Pax will be here tomorrow and you can be on your way. Keep thinking about that and you won't be afraid."

"Should I be afraid?" She asked the question to hear his deep voice again, the slow Western drawl curling around the warm room. Harmony had never been frightened since she first discovered her powers, she realized suddenly. Jonah didn't frighten her now; she wanted to touch her lips to the hard line of his. She ached to smooth his rumpled hair.

Harmony felt slow heat rise up her throat and, to her horror, Jonah studied her rising blush impassively. Then he began to eat. Harmony ate slowly, very aware of her uncertain emotions about Jonah.

Jonah Fargo stirred her as no other man had. To a woman who preferred elegance and simplicity and grace, Jonah's raw urgency acted like lightning racing across her taut nerves. Graceful, strong and dangerous, as though he spared nothing once his mind was locked to a purpose, his movements were too swift.

He stood abruptly and looked down at her. Heartbeats stretched by as she sensed Jonah's need to pick her up and carry her into the bedroom. He was a man of action, a man who took what he wanted...

Harmony fought the stirring within her, the fiery need to meet him recklessly on that white, hot plane. The air simmered with lightning and thunder between them. Harmony realized that her hand had risen protectively to her throat where her blood pulsed wildly, heavily. She looked away, stunned by her emotions and the sudden shyness that she had never experienced. The tiny bells on her bracelet jingled musically as she flattened her hands on the table, needing the solid wood to stop them from trembling.

She wasn't a shy woman, nor was she extremely sensuous. Yet now, with Jonah standing over her...

"The soup was good. I'm not much on herbs, so it suited me fine. Thank you," he said stiffly. "Leave the dishes. I'm used to doing things myself. Just don't mess anymore. I like things the way they are."

"Mess?" she asked incredulously. While Harmony recognized his appreciation of the meal, she resented his current attitude. *Ugh...woman obey man*—that darned elemental plane again where he nettled her as no other man had. She parted her lips to tell him that he just might not get a Santa Claus stocking this year. Then the wind began to howl mournfully and Jonah tilted his head, his body tense as he listened.

Shrimp immediately leapt to her feet and padded to Jonah, leaning against his legs as though to comfort him. Jonah closed his eyes and the light caught his black lashes, tipping them in blue sparks. The father's heart inside Jonah bled, aching for the daughter he'd cradled in his arms and who had made his life joyous and full. The empty Christmas seasons without Grace weighed too heavily upon him, like cold bricks. He breathed slowly, his expression one of deep pain, before he slowly opened his eyes to look down at Harmony. "You're safe and warm," he repeated. "Remember that if I seem a little strange tonight," he said to comfort her. He looked as though he were tearing apart and the pieces were flying away into the freezing wind.

The healer in her ached to help him. Harmony realized instantly that Jonah had the ability to send her emotions teetertottering. She stepped back, waiting for Jonah to sort through his problems.

Jonah's thoughts were controlled now, veering toward June Fields. Harmony straightened. She refused to be a mental participant of another romantic interlude between Jonah and his sexual medication. When she began to rapidly clear the table and wash the dishes, Jonah shrugged, and pulling on his coat, left the house, entering the howling wind as though it were his old friend.

From the steamy kitchen window, Harmony watched him lean into the force of the wind until he disappeared in a curtain of snow.

Come back... come back and stay warm, Jonah, she whispered silently. Jonah had sensed her need of the missing herbs; the man's psychic abilities lurked, prowling through his mind without his knowledge.

Harmony shivered slightly; she didn't envy Jonah's discovery, for it was a time of terror.

Later, when she placed the folded laundry in the old dresser, she found the doll. Resting in a worn box, the baby doll seemed new and unloved.

Harmony ran trembling fingers across the old box, then carefully lifted the doll free. She smoothed the worn lacy gown and held the doll close to her, sensing—big, work-roughened hands had trembled, smoothing the gown, cherishing the doll. Tears had dampened the cloth—Jonah had lost a child, a daughter.... The cry carried by the wind into Jonah's mind had been his memory of his daughter's—

Then a door slammed and Jonah's boots hit the worn linoleum, crossing to the bedroom where she stood. *He had loved his daughter so deeply. She was the reason he breathed, he laughed....*

"What are you doing?" Jonah asked roughly, the stark light hitting his rugged face, gleaming on the taut skin over his jutting cheekbones.

Harmony placed the doll aside on the dresser and moved into his arms, holding him closely. For an instant his pain caught her, a terror within him squeezing, hurting.... She gasped as the vise tightened in her own chest.

His heart raced beneath her cheek; he tensed, then a shudder moved down his body. "What's this?" he asked unevenly, in a hoarse whisper.

Harmony reached to lay her hand along his cheek, to take his pain and give him peace. But Jonah's head lifted back immediately, a proud man refusing comfort. Then his arms closed slowly around her, locking her to his body.

She knew then that Jonah Fargo would keep what he held dear.

He lifted her, until their eyes were level. "Jonah..." Harmony whispered before his lips touched hers gently.

She'd wanted to ease him for the moment, to take his pain into herself—but Jonah's lips were searching hers softly, teasingly, warmly, and Harmony let herself drift in unfamiliar, pleasing sensations.... She felt as if tiny warm ribbons were stroking her, cradling her gently against him.

Then Jonah's arms tightened, his hands opening wide to heat her back; his mouth changed, firmly demanding more than she wanted to give.

He was too close, too hard and too dangerous. His heat enveloped her, his needs driving against her. She glimpsed flames dancing on the honed edge of a sword....

"No," Harmony whispered against his lips and regretted the shiver that slid through her body. He continued to hold her, his mind foraging for answers. "No," she repeated, aware that her stocking feet were dangling inches above the floor. The tiny bells jingled as she pressed her hands against his hard chest; his heart was racing as wildly as hers.

"Lady, I'm not so old and so far gone that I don't recognize an invitation," Jonah said slowly. "Or a tease."

She didn't fear him, Harmony realized suddenly. She feared the need within herself to take the sweet, wild fire that Jonah's first kisses had offered. She fought the second shiver—stunned by her rising temper—as Jonah slowly lowered her to the floor.

"A tease?" she repeated unevenly, pushing back the building anger that he alone could raise in her.

His smile was not kind. "Try the cupid act on someone who is buying. You're not the first woman to think you can—"

"Think I can do what?" Harmony's hands curled into fists at her side. The bells tinkled.

"Have me. To think you can sweep a poor widower off his feet by feeding him and then treating him to honey kisses and curves," Jonah finished flatly. "Well, lady. You have picked the wrong cowboy. I am not in the mood for a tease or for a sweetheart. You'll have to contain your hugging urges until you can find someone more accommodating. The next time you grab me, you'd better mean business."

"You insufferable, low-down, uncivilized—" Harmony stopped abruptly, stunned that she had lashed out angrily at him. She instantly placed her fingers over her lips.

"Brute?" he asked mildly and a slow, amused gleam darkened his brilliant eyes. "Now that really hurts me. Just slashes me into tiny pieces."

Harmony inhaled and took a step backward, her back coming against the wall as Jonah loomed over her. She fought to think—his pain was defused, temporarily shadowed by his other emotions. He was focused on her now, and Harmony did not like being the object of his amusement. "I would not want you in my Christmas stocking if you came with a ton of gold and half a ton of diamonds," she stated.

"Uh-huh," Jonah murmured, flicking the gold cupid between her breasts with the tip of his finger. "You want to know what I think about Christmas stockings? They have big holes in them, and holiday cheer is so much hogwash. Stick to your cupids if you want romance, Miss Harmony Davis. I don't play games."

"Games?" He'd accused her of being a tease and a flirt. The taut silence stretched between them as Harmony thought of slapping him. She'd never lifted her hand in anger to anyone, but Jonah Fargo was asking for—

"Are you going to slap me or not?" he demanded.

Shrimp began to whine softly and came to stand between them.

Jonah's darkened gaze lowered down Harmony's body, then rose slowly. "You're a big girl, Harmony. You come at a man like that and he's going to get ideas. Now, what's it going to be? That bed and me, or a nice quiet evening where you stay in your corner and I stay in mine?" he asked slowly.

Harmony ignored the trembling of her fingers. She blinked in surprise, experiencing a wild urge to lock her fingers around his muscled neck and squeeze slowly. "I was consoling you, you jerk. Not making a move on you," she stated sharply.

"Uh-huh." His agreement lacked sincerity. "You call it what you want, and I'll call it something else. I never asked for your sympathy."

While Harmony dealt with her surprising anger, Jonah continued, "Put the doll back in the dresser and leave it alone. Come on, Shrimp. Let's leave the lady to ignite, because that's what she surely looks like she's going to do in another minute. When you settle down, Miss Harmony, open the door. You'll need the heat from the other room. I won't bother your pretty little warm body."

"Ugh," she muttered flatly, curling her fingers into fists. "Ugh. You speak, I obey."

He frowned. "What's that?"

"Just a bit of my Christmas cheer shattering under your boots."

Shrimp plopped to the floor and rested her muzzle on her front paws. She looked woefully up at her master as though he'd failed the simplest test. Jonah frowned at the dog, and then the bedroom door closed quietly behind him.

A second later, Harmony placed her fingers over her mouth to quiet a surprised yelp. She had just discovered that she had hopped onto the old creaking bed and had hurled both pillows at the closed door.

The lady was hopping mad.

Jonah listened to the silence of his house now that Harmony's bedsprings had stopped squeaking. He'd had enough experience to recognize the sound of a restless body flip-flopping on the old bed. He eased from his rocking chair and opened the bedroom door to allow the heat to enter the room. She might be too stubborn, but he wouldn't want to explain her pneumonia to Pax.

His hand tightened on the doorknob before he forced his fingers to slide away. Jonah inhaled slowly, catching a drift of her fragrance. He allowed himself to circle it, test the unfamiliar scent.

That warm, soft, woman scent.

He stood watching the flames in the stove's small window. The firelight slid across the linoleum to touch his bare feet. Maggie, his wife, had had cold feet. Maybe all women did.

What did he know about other women? Maggie had been all he'd wanted after his marriage; before their love he'd floundered once or twice.

Harmony moved gracefully, like a dancer, flowing across the floor rather than walking. Her hands moved like swaying willows in the gentle wind, yet she was a strong woman, the delicate muscles moving beneath her sweater and jeans.

The shadows of the bedroom called to him. When she was angry, the tiger woman leapt in her. Then she was soft, very soft, hurling herself into his arms with huge, tearful golden eyes.

When her emotions ran to caring, that generous rosebud mouth fit her face, the softness gently merging.

Jonah stroked his chin with his fingers. He remembered holding her—all those wild, springy curls were fragrant and silky-soft as he had rested his chin on the top of her head.

He moved from her flowery, exotic scents into the living room. He shook his head, disliking the softening running in him now, the longing for Christmas as it was when Grace laughed. He dislodged and shucked free of the troublesome woman as he removed his outer clothing down to his shorts.

Inhaling impatiently, Jonah eased onto the sagging, uncomfortable couch. He preferred the squeaking, lumpy affair to a bed because it kept him from sleeping.

His eyes were dry, gritty from the need for sleep, yet Jonah stared at the firelight dancing on the ceiling. When a man clung to sanity by his fingertips, sleep could make him vulnerable to dreams. He inhaled sharply, remembering the cupids he thought were tumbling, laughing, rolling on his knee and flying around his hat.

The woman made cupids and that had probably set him off, he reasoned. That and the gleaming gold cupid resting over her breasts. If he could lay his head on those soft round shapes, he could sleep and rest. Could a woman be erotic and sweet? he wondered. A tiger and a rosebud?

"I'm just a brick shy of a full load," Jonah muttered, to hear the reassuring sound of his own voice and to silence the soft sigh of the sleeping woman in the next room. "Jingle bells and cupids. Now that's a fine mix for a crazy cowboy."

A woman's scent, the memory of soft kisses and a warm curved, female body disturbed him. The taste of her lingered on his lips. He'd wanted to dive into her softness, to wallow in Miss Harmony Davis.

The couch creaked as he flipped a heavy quilt over himself. When a woman tasted like sweet honey, her lips pushing shyly against his, a man naturally got ideas.

There was something else. She disturbed his mind and it was tilted enough already. For a moment when she held him, Jonah's taut nerves eased and he sensed a homecoming.

Her eyes haunted him—the specks darkening, filling the tawny shade. Or when her temper rose, her eyes became hard and glittering like flashing gold disks. While her lips had tasted sweet, Miss Harmony had a real temper brewing from the set

of her jaw and the tender little pulse along her throat. Just for
an instant, when Harmony lost her Christmas cheer and glared
up at him as though she wanted to launch into him, Jonah felt
like smiling.

"Herbs," he muttered. When did he start thinking about
potted chives and parsley on window shelves? The thoughts
were peaceful, gentling and Jonah allowed his heavy lids to
close. He trusted the elements, the seasons and the hard facts
of ranch life, not the disturbing calm he'd felt in her arms, or
the restlessness of his thoughts when she was near. Harmony
Davis—city woman, cupid maker and jingle bell ringer—could
just take her Christmas cheer someplace else.

Jonah leapt to his feet as the dish crashed against the wall.
He wasn't sleeping now, wrapped in his terrifying nightmares
and the sound of the child crying.

He pushed his fingers through his hair, his hands gripping his
head as another dish smashed against the wall. His heart beat
wildly, rapidly, the sound of it galloping across his mind.

The child's sobs were so aching, so longing.

He breathed deeply, aching for his daughter. He realized
suddenly that he had yelled a curse and that Shrimp had
barked.

The woman was looking up at him, her face pale in the mass
of long, tawny-copper curls, her eyes huge and worried. Bells
tinkled as she reached to stroke his cheek, and he caught her
scent swirling around him.

"Jonah? It's Harmony. Jonah, you are dreaming," she said
in a low, soothing voice, her hand opening to rest softly on his
cheek.

Jonah brushed the unfamiliar touch aside; he had all he
could handle now with the child crying and the dishes smashing.

He shuddered, caught in the vise.

"Jonah?" she asked softly, stepping nearer to him, lifting
her hand again to touch his cheek.

"Don't touch me," he whispered unevenly, realizing distantly that he had to protect her from the rages within himself.

Her fingertips smoothed his temple and her eyes were soft, caring, warm.... "You won't hurt me, Jonah. Shh. Don't worry."

"I'm—" How could he tell her he was losing his mind?

"Shh," she soothed, the bells on her wrist creating a gentle music as she lifted her other hand to smooth his temple.

"You're—" He wanted to tell her that she was safe. That even in his worst moment, he would not hurt her.

"Safe," she whispered softly, her fingers creating slow, magic easing of the pain in his mind. "Jonah, you're unsettled because the New Year always brings memories of those we love. You need rest to deal with what is in you—you need to sleep now. I want you to think of the summer wind moving through the wheat, slowly...slowly. Can you do that?" she asked.

He realized his hands had locked in her hair, the soft silky warmth tethering him away from the abyss—he pictured the heavy heads of golden wheat, the wind creating waves like an ocean.

"That's it," she encouraged softly. "Waves like an ocean."

He clung to the gentler images, fighting the rage within him—he had lost a daughter...he had never given her the doll she wanted so much...where was Grace's Christmas doll...?

Where was he? His mind hovered between dreams and reality. His fingers tightened in her hair, crushing it desperately.

Harmony. His fingers smoothed the shape of her head now, the curls tethering him gently to her. Harmony was real. Soft. Warm. He allowed himself to wallow in her scent. Flowers. Spring running green across the mountains...Christmas and giving and loving.... So sweet...shy...warm...

"Jonah, you have to listen to me," Harmony said quietly, firmly.

Her body warmed his. He'd been so alone, too cold for too long. His hand found the nape of her neck, stroking it. Soft skin. Soft woman. Gentle, loving heart.

She moved restlessly beneath his touch, the shape of her shoulders firm within the cup of his hands. Harmony was real.

Jonah shook his head, dislodging her fingers, and rage leapt to the doorstep of his mind. "What are you doing?" he asked roughly, stepping away from her and shuddering with his emotions. She took a step toward him and his hand slashed the air between them, warning her to stay away from him. He didn't understand what was happening—who was this woman? Why could her touch calm his mind?

She frowned, her exquisite long fingers smoothing the hair he had just held. Harmony's eyes were filled with sympathy.... He didn't need anyone's pity. If he were going over the edge, he would do it by himself.

He looked down her body, his gaze moving over the T-shirt clinging to her breasts before falling to midthigh, then the long pale length of her legs. Who was she? What did she know? Why did she disturb his thoughts?

Why had dishes smashed against the wall? Why was he chatting mentally with Shrimp? Why? Why? Jonah turned away from the woman, seeking the safety of what he understood—loneliness, quiet.... He breathed deeply, painfully. He glanced at the broken dishes, praying that he had dreamed them smashing against the wall. The pieces lay on the floor, evidence that they had flown. Had he thrown them in his sleep?

Her hand touched his back, tethering him to a tenuous calm. He shrugged it away, desperate for answers.

"I know. You're frightened, fearing you are losing your mind. But those dishes really did hit the wall and, Jonah, you did not throw them in your sleep," Harmony stated softly behind him. "Jonah, your subconscious and your conscious mind are very troubled. You may have broken those dishes by... by movement of objects without physical contact. It's called psychokinesis."

Taking a deep breath, Harmony continued, "Jonah, please listen carefully. I believe you have powers."

"Powers?" He rubbed his temples impatiently. Why had Harmony's touch eased the tempest within his head?

"You sense things and there are images in your mind. If you concentrate, you could develop your psychic powers. Jonah, I think you have ESP, extrasensory perception," she repeated slowly.

Jonah tossed away her statement, then was slowly drawn back to it. "Psychic? ESP? Sounds better than crazy, lady." Then with an oh-hell attitude, Jonah said tightly, "You want to know why I'm nuts, lady? It's called guilt. My wife died when our daughter, Grace, was born. That was bad enough. Then Grace died in a blizzard five years ago. She was just eight. I never had a chance to give her the doll she wanted. Maybe if I would have given it to her that night, she would have—"

He swallowed, emotion tightening his throat. "Maybe Grace would have stayed inside the pickup, played with her doll...and she'd be thirteen and alive right now."

After running his shaking hands through his hair, Jonah turned to look at Harmony. Layers of control were ripping away from him, his painful scars giving way to fear. For a man who rarely talked, Jonah heard himself asking, "You want to know about powers? Harmony—Miss Cupid Maker, Miss By-Gosh, Isn't Christmas Great? For the last six months, I can hear a child cry in my mind!"

He waited for her reaction and eased back from her hand. He didn't want her to touch him. "Well? Tell me I'm crazy. Or run off to your room and lock the door. Go on. Do it. Do anything but cut that extrasensory perception bull."

Harmony inhaled slowly and squared her shoulders. "I understand your pain. But your anger and frustration is causing the dishes to fly through the air. I know, Jonah, because I have powers, too. It was painful discovering that I was so different from the other children. From other teenagers."

He stared at her, disbelieving.

Jonah, be kind to yourself. He shook his head, dislodging the thought that had slipped into his mind.

Swami, mystic bunk! he thought instantly and watched Harmony frown slowly.

I refuse to be angry with you. I understand your grief and your fears....

He slashed away the sense of kindness and sympathy with a curse. Her hands curled into tight fists as her frown deepened. "If you say that again, Jonah Fargo, I may just do something I'll probably regret."

"Listen here, little sweetheart, I've regretted many things, but telling you to keep your malarkey to yourself isn't one of them."

"'Little sweetheart'?" she repeated in an uneven, ominous tone.

"Little darlin'," Jonah corrected in a low drawl. The arch of his eyebrow and the slow, mocking curve of his lips dared her.

Three

───

She wouldn't let him get to her—she wouldn't—Harmony promised just before she cast cupids all over Jonah's tall, rigid body.

She pictured the cherubs tugging at his worn boxer shorts and skidding down his broad bare shoulders. She sent one sliding down his nose; she studied his body, taut, muscled stomach, a lithe, lean man, with muscles toned by hard work, angular—

Harmony stiffened when she discovered that she wanted to nestle against him.

His eyes widened slowly and he straightened. She couldn't help smiling grimly at his surprised expression, the fierce glowering warlord surrounded by fluttering little pink cherubs.

He closed his eyes and luscious June popped into Harmony's mind. "Jonah, sex with June won't help. Don't be brickminded. You have emerging powers, and I am getting a bit angry with your refusal to consider psychic existence," she warned him. "At least, consider the possibility."

He'd sealed her away from his thoughts, but she tensed as his smoldering gaze took in her body. Harmony crossed her arms over her chest, suddenly reminded that all she wore was Jonah's T-shirt and her briefs.

Shrimp hopped up on the couch and looked from Jonah to Harmony. The dog's ears lifted with keen interest in the shifting tension and mood in the room.

"Mmm," Jonah was saying appreciatively in a deep, husky, sexy voice as he considered Harmony's body from head to toe. "Would you like to hug me like you did before?" he invited in a tone that caused Harmony to shiver.

Not that she didn't know a man's sensual needs. Not that she hadn't been married and had experienced lovemaking—to a mild degree. Not that she hadn't been held closely against a lover.

Harmony took a step backward and jumped when she bumped into the old rocker. It creaked back and forth while she considered Jonah's expression. It was definitely that of a hungry male sighting down on a desirable woman.

Harmony blinked. Desirable? Her?

Her back met the wall and Jonah moved gracefully, firmly, through the night shadows toward her. He placed his hands on either side of her head, looking down at her quietly. "You kiss sweet," he said slowly, thoughtfully. "Like a rose dipped in dew."

She shivered, her breasts bumping gently into his chest. She inhaled instantly, the hard warm surface exciting, stirring her as never before.

Then his hard thigh moved between hers, nudging her softness gently and he said, "Forget that ESP malarkey. There's no such thing. I don't have it and I don't want it. I believe in what's real. And that's you and me and now."

Jonah's fingertip stroked her cheek, slowly traced the shape of her lips and slid over her chin. The delicate, sensual pressure trailed to her cupid charm. "Well?" he asked deeply.

She shivered, unable to look away from Jonah's dark gaze. He wanted her. He wanted to bring her lips and body against his and demand everything. Her throat tightened, causing her voice to lower huskily. "Well?" she repeated. "Well...what?"

"I haven't been kissed in a long time," Jonah returned, his gaze easing from her lips and down her body. "You are one lush lady, Harmony."

Harmony blinked and straightened, trying on her "lush-lady" and "good-kisser" suit. It didn't fit. It never had. Her body was tall and strong. She was a bit too broad through her shoulders; her muscles were defined by hard physical work. Filled with an unfamiliar ache, she refused to consider the round firm shape of her breasts. They weren't spectacular, pert or unusual. She considered her shape as matronly at best—compact, healthy, with hips and thighs that gathered inches like a magnet gathered iron.

Jonah stood there, simmering in his hungry male juices and waiting to pounce. She refused to shiver one more time, her body's needs lurching precariously toward what he offered. The only conclusion she gathered was that Mr. Lonesome for June was making a play for the only woman in his vicinity. Harmony had never been a substitute player, nor did she intend to be. She blew away the curl that had been bouncing gently against her temple as she tapped her foot. "Because you are standing there in your shorts and I am standing here in your T-shirt does not pave the way for a romantic interlude, Mr. Fargo."

He leaned to nuzzle her hair gently. Harmony stood very still, her emotions uncertain. "Who said anything about romance?" he asked softly against her temple. "We're a little old for that silliness, aren't we?"

Harmony shivered, but refused to retreat, concentrating on holding her unfamiliar anger in check. She'd always faced everything life threw at her, including her powers. They were past the Christmas-cheer area and into another basic realm; Jonah Fargo needed a lesson about women and sensitivity, and she was just the one to give it to him.

He lifted his head to look down at her. "Why don't you just go ahead and explode and do whatever you think you're going to do? Then maybe we can both get some sleep."

Jonah knew he had gotten to her. From the smirk on his dark, bearded face and the gleam in his blue eyes surrounded by tiny crinkling lines, she saw that he enjoyed getting to her. He relished causing her anger to go TILT in big red letters. "I could devastate you," Harmony managed unevenly, distantly aware that she had never threatened anyone in her life. "I could take that tiny, one-track brain of yours and—"

"Uh-huh. Sure. I'm scared. You say you've got powers. You think I've got them. Why don't you throw a mind brick at me and see if I can catch it?" Jonah said, his grin widening as he crossed his arms over his chest and stood back. His stance, that of an arrogant male challenging her as no other man had ever done, caused Harmony to study her trembling, splayed fingers. It was better than wrapping them around his throat.

A distant, but firm realization hovered around her shimmering anger—when Jonah was tormenting her, she acted blindly and her powers were overridden, her emotions and her body responding without the control she had always exercised....

From the couch, Shrimp whined softly, apologizing for her master.

Harmony closed her eyes, fighting for the control that Jonah did not deserve. He was standing there in his boxer shorts, a hole in the material covering his right thigh, his upper body tanned darkly and his long muscled legs pale, and he was challenging her—

Why, you... Then she pictured the dinosaur teeth lifting off the table into the air; the huge array of petrified teeth hovered in the air and laughed. Next, Harmony raised a cupid army to decorate Jonah like a Christmas tree. A tiny angel fluttered to rest on his rumpled black hair and held up a sprig of mistletoe. In a dash of inspiration, Harmony packaged Jonah in a big red satin ribbon and tagged him with a huge sign that read Warning. Overheated Male. Do Not Open Until Christmas. Use Extreme Caution When Unwrapping.

He stood very still, his hands curled into fists, watching her as she crossed her arms and smiled grimly. "Now you're ready for June. Tell me aloud what you are wearing, Jonah." Then she pictured him in ruffled shorts decorated with jingle bells and cupids. To prompt him, she placed the sound of reindeer hoofbeats on his rooftop.

"Shorts," he said between his teeth, scowling at her. He tilted his head, a characteristic she recognized when Jonah was listening carefully.

She caused Dancer and Prancer to do a fast jig, and Jonah glanced at the ceiling warily. He dusted away the cupid toying with the lace at his thigh, lifting it slightly to peek— Jonah slapped his open hand flat against his thigh. "Just shorts," he repeated very firmly.

"June will love your outfit," Harmony singsonged.

"Do you?" he tossed back at her with a rakish grin.

Because her life usually ran as smoothly as her name, Harmony was unused to fast repartee or volatile men. Or the sensual gleam that lighted the tough cowboy's eyes. Usually men looked at her as a good friend, or as an artist, or simply as a marketing person doing her job. Jonah's steady, intense look reminded her of steam and storms and heat. She resented the hair lifting at the nape of her neck. "Now is not the time to torment me, Mr. Hot to Trot."

"No one ever crosses you, do they?" he asked slowly, as though turning his thoughts very carefully. "You don't like anything disturbing your life and what you want, do you? Everything and everyone just march as you want, right? If something—someone—gets too close, you just ease away, don't you?"

He'd struck too close, dancing into her life and opening corners she wanted to leave dusty and in the past. She didn't like arguing and she'd never tasted the need for revenge as poignantly as now. Harmony breathed quickly as carolers began to sing in the snowstorm she had created in the cabin. She tucked a Christmas tree into a corner and a roasting turkey in the oven. Fresh pumpkin pies sat on the counter.

Harmony studied her revenge-prey closely. Sweat gleamed on his forehead and on his upper lip. His hands formed tight fists, the knuckles pale beneath dark skin. "Tell me what you are wearing," she ordered again in a taut whisper.

Jonah closed his eyes and frowned. Harmony saw herself in a transparent black baby-doll negligee, an item she had never owned. A huge Christmas bow that ran from her shoulder across her breast to her hip slowly unraveled. The silky negligee began to slide slowly upward as though being removed by a man's hand. She tugged the image down, then crossed her arms over her breasts. Though Jonah did not recognize his powers, they were developing too rapidly for her taste. "I never wear sexy nightgowns," she stated baldly.

"Maybe you should. It's a sight a man appreciates, especially that little mole right—"

She slapped her hand over her left breast, shielding the tiny mole. As an afterthought, she placed her other hand over the small strawberry birthmark on her right buttock—which was covered by an image of tiny transparent and ruffled briefs.

Shrimp tilted her head inquiringly as she looked at Harmony.

Jonah smiled wolfishly then, looking very pleased, and then horror spread across his expression. "I...am...losing my mind," he said shakily and walked slowly to the couch.

Jonah Fargo had aged in heartbeats and she had been a part of his pain. She'd pushed him too hard, too soon, before he was ready to realize. Horrified at the consequences of her dark temper, Harmony watched him ease onto the couch like an elderly man.

Jonah sat with his head bent and his eyes closed. Then he turned haunted eyes to her, the shadows waiting for him, ready to enclose him in nightmares and loneliness. Harmony instantly regretted her loss of control. She had done this terrible thing to him, added to his uncertainty, his anguish. Harmony had never hurt anyone in her lifetime, and she knew instantly that tonight Jonah would hear the child's sobbing again. Her anger had strengthened his powers and increased his awareness—even now his desperation shrouded him, a man clinging to reality by his fingertips and she had nudged him....

"I don't know what's happening to me," he murmured tiredly, the lines deepening in his face. "Go on to sleep now, Miss Harmony. It's only—" he glanced at the clock and his expression said he'd lived ten lifetimes "—almost two o'clock now. Pax will be here tomorrow and you'll be fine. You can wallow in all the Christmas cheer you want."

He slowly rested his head on the back of the couch, his face lined and harsh. "Go on. Get some rest," he said in a deep, hollow tone as though he knew the morning would find him dry-eyed and sleepless. As though he knew his tomorrows would be filled with the sound of the child crying....

She almost cried out her apologies, but realized that one more mental fling would only serve to bring Jonah closer to his abyss. "You will sleep tonight, Jonah Fargo," she promised softly when she lay in bed.

* * *

Jonah stretched and yawned sleepily and the bed creaked gently beneath him. He stopped moving, then tested the freshly laundered sheets with his toes. He slowly crushed the pillow with his fingers. He'd fallen asleep on the uncomfortable couch....

Dreams. Good dreams curled around him, soothing touches, whispers, the softness enclosing him, relaxing him. Jonah kept his eyes closed, trying to stay in the dreams, wrap them around him for just a while longer....

Hands had touched his forehead gently, fingers stroking his temples and brow, soothing him. There had been a loving family enclosing him—a woman, children, a man had smiled at him. He was a part of them, sharing, loving...

Warm. He'd been warm last night, safe, comfortable, his heart and mind at ease. He'd felt a healing, his heart mending....

The child had not cried out to him....

He remembered last night. Anger darkened Harmony's magnificent eyes, the storms swirling around her as he denied having psychic abilities. *He'd worn lace boxer shorts decorated with jingle bells and cupids. He had imagined the sound of reindeer hooves on his rooftop.*

Jonah breathed lightly, and one glance at the window told him that he had slept heavily. The day was brilliant, blinding, the sunlight intensified by the snow. The wall clock chimed softly—seven o'clock, well past his waking hour when he was able to sleep.

He caught a scent—flowers in a spring meadow, sunlight and morning dew. Then a subtler, erotic touch of a woman—Harmony Davis.

Jonah rose quickly to his feet. He slid into his jeans, then walked quickly to Harmony's room. Shrimp, curled on the rug beside her bed, looked up at him with an expression that said he should hush; Harmony had had a bad night.

Harmony sprawled across the bed on her stomach, the bells on her wrist catching the morning night. Jonah bent, crouching beside the bed to study her—his Christmas-happy intruder. He smiled slightly, surprising himself, when he thought of how magnificent she had been, pitting herself against him, head lifted and amber eyes flashing.

He slid a fingertip beneath the curls covering her cheek and eased them gently away.

Her face was pale, dark bruises circling her eyes. Harmony Davis looked like a woman who had spent the night at the bedside of a needy friend. On the nightstand rested a plate dusted with biscuit crumbs.

Jonah found his hand touching hers, his fingers curling around the slender, capable feminine ones. He owed her an apology; he'd never behaved with a woman like he had behaved with Harmony last night. His thumb stroked the fine inner skin of her wrist, testing the slow pulse there as he considered his apology. To a man living alone, words didn't come easy.

Then he was looking into Harmony's haunted eyes. She stared blankly at him for a moment, weariness swirling in the soft depths.

"Were you hungry last night?" he asked, unwilling to spread her crazy notions about psychic abilities into the momentary peace he had been feeling.

"Mmm. Hungry. I ate the rest of the biscuits." Her voice was drenched in sleep. Jonah couldn't stop his eyes from skimming down the quilts covering her. How many years ago had he awakened to a woman's scent? To the soft warmth?

Harmony's eyes closed slowly as she clung to sleep. She had not been as tired last night, and now she was exhausted. Harmony stretched beneath the quilts and yawned. "Sorry. I'll make breakfast in a minute. I'm a nervous eater. Comes from childhood problems and—"

Suddenly those magnificent, dark golden eyes opened to his and her fingers tightened on his. "When I began to discover my abilities— Jonah, did you sleep well?"

"If you're gearing up to toss that psychic malarkey at me— don't," Jonah ordered, unwilling to leave her touch, yet sensing she wanted to talk about his so-called powers.

She'd touched him in the night—while he slept. She'd given him peace. He remembered a gentle touch, the taut agony flowing out of him. He shook his head, trying to clear the sound of her soft, beckoning voice. Impossible! The images were only proof that he was sliding.

"You think you hear Grace crying for her doll, Jonah."

Jonah eased his fingers away and stood as Harmony drew the quilts to her chest and sat up. Her face was stark and pale in the shadows of the room.

"Doll?" Jonah thought of the baby doll he planned to give Grace. The doll that he had cradled in his worst moments, remembering how badly she'd wanted it. The doll his tears had dampened.... He was angry then for allowing himself to come near Harmony this morning, to feel the softness that could only turn into pain. "Lady, I had a real taste of your nutty ideas last night. You need help," he stated flatly before walking out of the bedroom.

Then, because he was raging, frustrated and fresh from having his pain spread before him, Jonah returned to stand over her bed. "You're mule-headed, Harmony. You've locked onto a dingbat idea, and I don't need any more buttons pushed right now. Or your misplaced sympathy."

He swallowed, the thought of Grace crying for her doll too painful, too impossible.... "Keep this mind-reading, crystal ball stuff away from me until Pax comes. Better yet—tell me what I'm thinking about now." He placed his hands on his hips and thought about making love to Harmony because that was truly what he wanted to do.

To make love to sweet Harmony until neither of them had the energy to think or move. The way he felt now, their loving season might last through to the New Year.

She flushed deeply, lifting the blankets to her chin. "Jonah, you should be ashamed of yourself."

"Why?" he asked innocently, then mentally spread Harmony's pale body over his darker one. If she wanted to think she could read his mind, she was in deep trouble. While she preferred to wallow in mental untruths, he had always moved quickly through life, doing what had to be done and not dwelling on anything but reality.

His physical reality now was sharp and drawn from a dream about Harmony wearing a skimpy nightgown. A tormenting sensual need tightened his muscles when he would have preferred to disregard the image. "Tell me what I'm thinking of now."

Heat. Storms. Hunger. Harmony locked to him, making love.

Her expression darkened. "I refuse to be involved, my fine buckaroo," she said.

"Right," Jonah said disbelievingly, satisfied that Harmony couldn't read his mind. Then he frowned slightly, sensing an emotion quivering in her. Was it fear? Fear for him? Fear of him? "Look. I apologize for last night. For the come-on. I've never wanted anyone but my wife."

The sunlight from the window touched her hair in a glossy halo and caught the angular set of her jaw. She sat there, wrapped in her stormy temper and the quilt, her earring hoops shimmering gold, knees drawn to her chest, and he wanted her.

Jonah ran trembling fingers through his hair. He'd made enough of a fool of himself last night. When a man clung to sanity by his fingertips, he didn't need a Gypsy woman tipping him over the edge. "I don't know what this ESP malarkey is. I don't have it. I don't want it. It's not real anyway. But, lady, you sure do know how to stir me up."

As he was leaving the room, walking quickly away from the unsettling emotions, her softly spoken words caught him in midstride. "Merry Christmas, Jonah. I'll see that you're repaid for saving my life."

"Leave it," he said for the second time since he'd met Harmony.

Four hours later, he wiped away frost from the barn window and watched Harmony. A small, trudging figure in the vast white plains, Harmony walked through the deep snow toward the highway where Pax had been honking.

The lady was trouble. Delicious trouble and too tempting for a man who was too old, too scarred. She wasn't pretty, but she unnerved his senses. No wonder he was seeing cupids and mistletoe and laughing dinosaur teeth ... Harmony Davis had stepped into his life, tossing her crazy ideas at him and filling his stomach with good food.

His mind was shifting, veering, remembering glimpses of her standing in his T-shirt. Or was it a black transparent negligee?

Nothing made sense anymore.

Harmony had said the sound he heard was in his mind—Grace crying for her doll. If he believed that, he was ready for the— Jonah remembered the image of himself standing in cupid-splashed shorts with mistletoe sprigs over his ears and the whole package tied with a big red bow.

Jonah shook his head, trying to shatter the image. Lack of sleep caused a man to think crooked.

Harmony had hugged him. Moved right into his arms and held him tight as though to comfort him. He'd acted like some yahoo, wanting her hungrily.

His body ached from the unfamiliar sensual tension even now. Her lips tasted like rose petals and dewdrops. Pax's little sister had a round, firm body that fit snugly against Jonah's rangy, lean one. She wasn't happy about him in her life, either. She liked easy people, comfortable, gentle ways. She enjoyed kissing and hugging from Pax's family, but she kept others at a safe distance. And unless he missed his guess, Miss Harmony didn't want entanglements of the heart any more than he did.

And unless he'd gone totally over the edge, in her lifetime Miss Harmony hadn't been touched as a real woman should be touched. With nothing between, no-holds-barred, and no holding back.

Jonah closed his eyes and pictured the round shape of her breasts beneath the transparent negligee. She had a tantalizing little strawberry birthmark on her right buttock. Those big, surprised honey-shaded eyes told him that no one had ever kissed her there. Those sweet lips alone could drive a man all the way over the edge. . . . She had that sweet, pure look that made a man want to cuddle her.

He'd been thinking of more than cuddling last night just after the cupid brigade got to him.

"Cupids. Get a grip on yourself, cowboy," Jonah said to himself as he bent to grip the pitchfork. "Making moves on a woman at your age could cause some real problems. Let alone a woman who believes in mind reading for real."

Jonah stopped in the middle of pitching hay to the horses, his leather gloves tightening on the handle.

June. Harmony had specifically said "June" before he had mentioned the name. How did she know?

He shook his head. Pax must have said something about June chasing Jonah. Jonah heard himself mutter, "Extrasensory powers. No way in hell."

Then the child began to whimper in the barn's shadows and Jonah sagged against the wall.

Harmony leaned her head against the pickup window and closed her eyes wearily. "I'm glad the moving van wasn't too difficult to get out of the snow," she said.

"A neighbor drove it to my ranch. I knew when you said Jonah had picked you up and that you were staying at his place, that you'd do this to yourself," Pax said quietly as he drove toward his ranch.

"Mmm," she murmured, too drained to nap. Jonah's wounding was deeper than she believed at first. He'd hovered in the shadows too long, clinging to memories and refusing to enjoy life, blaming himself for Grace's death. He'd cherished his daughter above himself.

"You took his pain, didn't you, Harmony?"

"He needed sleep."

"And you didn't? You could have rested, or asked me to help you."

"You wouldn't have wanted to know Jonah's thoughts last night," she muttered.

"He's on the edge. Janice and I have been trying to get him to visit, but Jonah doesn't want to intrude." Pax looked sharply at Harmony. "Jonah Fargo caused you to lose your temper? You threw cupids on him and he looked cute in lace shorts with mistletoe tucked over his ears? He wore a big red bow?" Pax asked incredulously.

Harmony flicked him an irritated look, then closed her eyes. She hadn't meant to think of Jonah like that. Pax's abilities were still active, but then he'd always been tapped into her thoughts. When they were young, he teased her at every turn—if he wasn't caring for her, protecting her from the cruelty of other children. "Lay off," she ordered mildly, then blanked her mind.

"Well . . . well," Pax murmured in a tone she didn't trust. "And you think he's sweet in a way, do you?" Then he began to laugh loudly and tears formed in his eyes.

Harmony thought of a big glass of ice water and dashed it on Pax. He shook his head, shivered and chuckled. "You just defended him. You can understand his grief and his guilt. This should be really interesting."

Pax hadn't lost his ability to torment her, she decided as she noted a passing coulee—a small ravine cut through the plains. Her brother had picked up one soft thought—how she could understand Jonah's grief—and threw it at her. "Jonah has powers, Pax. They are emerging and he's edgy. That's the only reason he thought of me as desirable. He's off center right now and not thinking clearly. He's a physical person who acts instantly and he's uncomfortable with deep thoughts."

"Jonah Fargo is the clearest-thinking man I know. He's got a mind that goes from A to B to C. He acts fast in critical situations, like jumping into the Missouri River to save a life when everyone else was planning and worrying. He saved a three-year-old boy last year. He's thorough and—"

"Toss sex-hungry and smirking in there someplace," she said too sharply. "All he could think about was some woman named June. I really didn't appreciate being a third party to his plans for the night. The steam was almost coming out his ears. It was disgusting."

Harmony refused to shiver one more time because of Jonah Fargo. She liked her life organized, smooth and without confrontations.

Jonah was a living confrontation if she ever saw one. She resented his thought that she was exotic and curvy and that he wanted to kiss the strawberry birthmark on her buttock and nuzzle her breasts. Mr. Little Sweetheart Fargo was a physically oriented man to her mental-contemplative personality. The equation was like that of water and oil.

His "little darlin'" remark had really stripped away her control. She gripped the bells on her wrist, staying the tiny jingles as her hand trembled. For just a moment before her cupid escapade—her first act of revenge—she'd wanted to fling herself at him.

Sensing thoughts other than her own, Harmony slammed down a mental curtain; Pax's lesser abilities needed slower thoughts and she refused to feed them to him.

"June has been after him for years. Jonah must be weakening," Pax stated thoughtfully.

"Not in some areas. You'd think he was half his age," Harmony muttered, fully awake now, anger tugging at her nerves. She tossed aside Jonah's steamy thoughts. He'd been confused, no doubt, aching for June.

What's age got to do with it? And, sis, you sound just a touch jealous of June.

Harmony leveled a stare at him and thought serenely, *Pax. Take a note. I do not want to think-chat about Jonah.*

"I hope you brought lots of chamomile tea," Pax murmured, not bothering to shield his grin. "I know you like a cup now and then to settle your nerves...and don't throw any more mental ice water on me. It's cold enough."

Four

Two weeks later, on Christmas Eve, Jonah kicked the snow from his boots. Snow spread endlessly into the moonlight, covering the wheat fields. The walkway leading to Pax's house had been meticulously shoveled, then swept.

In the light from the lamppost, Jonah's boots still looked scuffed, though he had polished them twice.

He closed his eyes. He was scuffed all over, tough as old leather. He dreaded the holiday season, and Christmas didn't fit into his world. Meeting Harmony hadn't helped. Dreaming about full-bodied women wearing see-through nighties had jarred him into another realm of problems.

Sweet as honey and tempting as melted butter over fresh-baked bread kisses hadn't helped, either. Jonah didn't want to think about what might have happened if she'd opened her mouth to him.

She out-and-out scared him; around her, he danced on the edge of excitement. He'd wanted to get under that smooth voice, that practiced grace and rev her motor like she was starting his.

He'd acted cocky as a kid and about as starved for woman flesh. And he'd invited her into his bed without sweet talk or a bouquet of flowers. Any woman, even an off-center one like Harmony, deserved better than his crude invitation.

Invitation? That was a lacy cover for his sleazy ultimatum. Jonah inhaled the freezing air, letting it cut into his lungs. She'd stood her ground and threw it back at him. He reluctantly admired her for that.

He released his breath. But it was something else, too. A fanciful need to linger in that sweet little girl's arms. *Sweet little girl,* he repeated mentally, reminded at once of how his father had lovingly called his mother, "sweet little girl." Harmony was more like a burr under Jonah's saddle. Her mind-reading ideas belonged in a carnival swami's tent.

Coincidences happened. Like when he desperately needed a distraction from the crying, just a few minutes to rest—Shrimp had pushed a chair to the radio on the kitchen counter and had leapt up to push the button. Jonah's favorite Motown music—the upbeat Temptations—had instantly spread through the house.

"Coincidence," he muttered. Things just happened at a time that paralleled Jonah's thoughts. Like wondering if Fancy Ledbetter, a seventeen-year-old neighbor, was taking good care of her barrel-racing pony. Then Fancy telephoned him about the pony's new tricks.

He glanced up at the holly wreath and twinkling lights over Pax Davis's door and inhaled. It was two weeks since he'd seen Harmony and he wasn't looking forward to this encounter. But Pax had called just after a book had turned to the page that Jonah had wanted; he hadn't touched the pages. Shaken by the event and blaming it on the house's drafts, he'd jumped at Pax's offer of spending Christmas Eve with the Davis family. After he hung up the phone, he remembered Harmony and how she and her weird ideas disturbed him. He'd had a nightmare of cupids fluttering around him and peeking up his shorts while he was awake and standing on his feet. Before the cupids bushwhacked him, he'd just gotten into the swing of tormenting her, watching her eyes glow like a tiger's; she was bristling nicely and he'd really started to enjoy his revenge for her invading his life.

Cupids. Her cupid necklace must have set him off, triggering some lost memory of Valentine's Day.

Jonah tightened his lips. Cupids weren't on the menu to-night. He would enjoy a good meal and maybe cuddle Pax's two little girls. He'd enjoy whatever boy treasures five-year-old Jimmy had to show him. Later, Janice would fix him a take-home sack of good food and he'd drive into Fort Benton and spend the night in a motel overlooking the old Missouri River. He'd even play Motown sounds as Shrimp's present. They'd share leftover turkey sandwiches and cherish Gladys Knight and the Pips, or maybe the Supremes. He might even do his imita-tion of Marvin Gaye, or dance like one of the Four Tops.

Anything but return to his empty house.

He was stretched so taut that he just thought he'd read other persons' thoughts. This past week had been especially bad. The last-minute shoppers in the department store were worrying about bills and if the Christmas turkey would feed everyone. A young mother hovered near the toys, wishing she could buy a nice doll for her daughter.

Lucky Halfpenny, who pictured himself as the local ladies' man, was thinking of ways to meet Pax's sister. Lucky worried about her favorite drink. He hoped it wasn't too expensive, but guessed that she might be worth the cost if she got really friendly. Lucky had stopped thinking and Jonah found that he had been glaring at him over the men's dress shirts. "New lady in town," Lucky had explained as he prowled through the shirts. "Not that you're interested in getting duded up for fe-males."

Lucky had glanced at Jonah carelessly before returning to his selection of a shirt. "Reckon you've worn those clothes for this century. May as well wear 'em into the next."

"Women like me for my charm," Jonah had muttered in his defense.

He was just counting the number of ironed patches on his best jeans when the salesclerk glanced at him. Jonah caught the impression that the clerk had envied Harmony's black crushed velvet dress with the low V-bodice. She'd worn it to a Christ-mas party the week before.

Lucky swooshed toward the checkout counter like a bandit ready to pounce. Harmony's black party dress sure was some-thing. He'd look good in the new pink shirt; Harmony would look good in it on the morning after, while she cooked his breakfast. After she did a load or two of his laundry, maybe he'd suck her toes. He worshiped full-bodied women like Harmony who could fill out V-necklines and whose nice soft breasts—

Lucky's leer was easily read by Jonah, though he wasn't a mind reader.

Because of her obvious devotion to Shep, Shrimp was the only dog allowed in the store. She had plopped down next to Jonah's boots and wondered dreamily what brand of dog food that Shep liked best—

Standing out in the cold night with the snow covered plains around him, the twinkle lights dancing up on Pax's rooftop, Jonah gritted his back teeth.

Jonah Fargo might be losing his mind, but he was no psychic, he thought as the door of Pax's home opened and a woman too tall to be Janice raced toward him. She crushed something bulky to her, four thick streamers flying from the bundle. Another short thick streamer coming from her head had a ball on the end of it.

"Behave, sweetheart," he ordered Shrimp as the collie raced past him, yipping happily as though greeting an old friend.

"Hi, and shush," Harmony whispered urgently to the dog. Then Shrimp grinned and Harmony hurriedly continued toward Jonah.

The shape of her legs below the sweaterlike dress momentarily distracted Jonah. He did appreciate a woman with strong legs—not bulky, but not that skinny, either.

"No," he stated. Then he backed up several steps as she continued toward him. His back hit the pickup as he gathered his presents for the Davises into one arm and stuck out a protective hand with the other. "No. I am not wearing that Santa Claus suit," he said firmly, startling himself.

Harmony stopped in front of him and tilted her head, sending a long, untamed spill of curls over her shoulder. "So, Jonah. If you can't read my thoughts, how did you know that I want you to wear this Santa Claus suit?" she challenged saucily with an I've-got-you smirk.

Jonah inhaled slowly. Just because she knew how to set him off, he wasn't admitting to imaginary powers. Living alone probably made him more sensitive to expressions and the movements of other people. Like a lone wolf picking up scents and sorting through them. Everything had a reason, Jonah reminded himself firmly as he said, "You running toward me...wearing a Santa hat and carrying a pillow...and the red suit decorated in white was a real clue. Black shiny fake boots like that don't leave room for error, lady."

He wanted to kiss her again. To pick her up and cuddle her on his lap in the pickup and steam up the windows, tasting her sweet-as-wildflowers-on-the-meadow kisses. She'd look pretty as a newborn calf in her black nightie and that Santa Claus hat. He must have moved toward her because she took a step backward. Then he realized he hadn't moved.

Shrimp was watching the humans with interest; Jonah sensed she was plotting something about later under the mistletoe.

"No," Harmony said firmly. "We're not repeating that scenario. You make one move on me, Jonah, and I'll—" She frowned and shook her head, thrusting the clothes at him. "You couldn't have known about the boots. They were hidden by the pillow. And how do you know they're fake anyway? They are just cover-ups, by the way. Put them over the top of yours. Don't argue. Just get into these clothes while I go get the children's presents from the barn."

"Give me one good reason why I should, boss lady." Jonah resented her waving his guesses in his face and proclaiming them to be evidence of sensory powers. In his lifetime, no one pushed Jonah Fargo. Maybe it was time that Harmony learned a lesson or two—

"You look awful, Jonah. Worse than when I met you," she said suddenly in a soft concerned tone, tilting her head to study him. Before Jonah could rap out a comeback, Harmony placed her hands along his cheeks, drew him down to her level and planted a gentle kiss on his lips. He glimpsed Christmas trees and happy children and loving families. "Take care of yourself, Jonah," she whispered before stepping back, her eyes luminous and huge in the dim light.

Jonah realized that little kept him from reaching out for her; he dug his fingers into the pillow. He swallowed and looked down at her, trying to find his balance and what he was going to say before she kissed him. He felt as if he were swaying in the freezing wind and Harmony was his only safety. Nettled because she caused emotions he didn't want or thoughts he didn't understand, Jonah drawled, "You need to control yourself, little sweetheart. A man gets ideas real quick when a woman kisses him."

Harmony's eyes widened momentarily, then narrowed ominously. "I don't have time to deal with you now, Jonah. So this is how it's going to be...."

She shook her head and closed her eyes as though she were about to leap over a cliff and should know better. Then she reached over the pillow and clothing in his arms to tug his head down to hers. With her soft mouth beneath his, Jonah went down like the proverbial ton of bricks. He saw excited children gathered around a twinkling Christmas tree, waiting to open their presents. He saw himself in a Santa Claus suit, making Pax's family very happy. He saw himself grinning with the sheer joy of living....

With the air of a woman who had just completed a difficult mission, Harmony stepped back from him. Jonah looked at her and knew that she'd done something contrary and suspicious to him. But he couldn't worry about that now, though, because Pax's family was waiting for Santa Claus.

"I didn't want to do that, but I was desperate," Harmony stated breathlessly. "I knew you wouldn't go down easy. The children are counting on Santa Claus and the pants won't fit over Pax's cast. He's not supposed to be on his feet anyway. The accident just happened this afternoon. He thought he could leap from the roof of one shed to another and missed. Just stuff yourself into this suit and try for a little Christmas spirit. Please," she added as an afterthought before she hurried toward the barn.

Jonah tried to focus on the rooftop's twinkle lights and remember what he was going to teach Harmony. He sniffed the cinnamony scent she'd swirled around him and wondered how she had netted and poleaxed him.

Shrimp looked anxiously up at Jonah. The beard that had dropped in the Santa Claus clothes shuffle dangled from her mouth. She was begging him to not be obnoxious and spoil her fun; they wouldn't be asked back and she was really tired of his company. Then Jonah received a notion that Shrimp wanted him to "go with the flow." She was asking him to make the

evening a pleasant one and not disgrace her. An obscure dog-
gie prayer slipped through Jonah's mind. It involved catching
Shep beneath the mistletoe and vamping him.

Jonah braced his back against the pickup and clutched the
costume and gifts in his arms while he tried to surface from
whatever hit him. Meanwhile, he watched Shrimp race after
Harmony. His eyes locked to the fast sway of Harmony's
rounded hips. Jonah's fingers clutched the soft pillow. She had
a real nice round backside.

Minutes later, he buckled the wide Santa belt. He adjusted
the pillow covering his stomach and mourned his life since he'd
met Harmony Davis. Within heartbeats of seeing her again, his
life was slanting at a disastrous pitch. As soon as was polite, he
was leaving for the safety of his motel room and Motown music. If he lived this night down, he'd hole up and decide what
to do about Miss Harmony Davis, with her nice backside and
her dingy ideas.

Harmony swirled her cinnamon stick in her hot apple cider
and studied the two cloves in the bottom of her glass cup. The
cloves didn't match, just like Jonah and herself.

At least cider-soaked cloves weren't combustible, she decided moodily, as she eased to sit on the arm of the sofa.

Harmony inhaled sharply, then stuck another homemade
beer-and-cheese stick in her mouth. Her nervous eating mal-
ady jumped into high gear when she thought of Jonah. She
shifted restlessly on the arm of the couch; she didn't like moods
and she wasn't going to be susceptible to Jonah's deep chuck-
les as the children crawled over his lap and he gifted them with
presents from his bag.

She'd been startled with her decision to zap Jonah into sub-
missiveness. She'd simply reached out, grabbed him and fogged
him with what she wanted him to do.

The warning bells on her bracelet seemed to be disarmed
when Jonah was near. Her senses, emotions and bodily impulses to attack him went into overdrive.

She swirled the two cloves and they nestled together in the
bottom of her cup. She sloshed the liquid gently to get the
cloves to separate, but they remained together, cuddling to-

gether in the hot, sweet cider like— Harmony discarded the word *lovers*.

She remembered Jonah's statement about her kiss. She hadn't "come at a man like that" so he'd "get ideas." Jonah had some weird idea that she'd kissed him because she wanted him.

Why would she want Jonah Fargo? A nasty-mannered, tall, time-battered, tough cowboy, with lightning and thunder eyes when they weren't smoky with dreams of her wearing a transparent black nightie... and a Santa Claus cap. His very own round, firmly packed Christmas present. He'd wanted to pick her up and lay her down on the pickup seat—

Right. As if any man could pick her up. Jonah certainly had big ideas and a real high opinion of his strength. He appreciated her round backside, like a potential buyer for a mare at auction.

She frowned and placed the empty cup aside as she remembered something else Jonah had thought at his house. She'd forgotten or dismissed it then, but now it surged into her mind. What was that he thought about "'tasting her sweet sassy mouth to shut her up'?"

Men had said she was classy, aloof, pleasant, easygoing, conservative and warm. They had never said anything about being sweet and sassy, and not one of them had pictured her in a black nightie.

And Pax had said Jonah wasn't a womanizer. Uh-huh. Right. That's why he presented Harmony with a vision of what he wanted to do with June. When he'd thought about kissing the birthmark on her buttock, Harmony had merely been in his vicinity; she'd been drenched in his excess of sensual-need residue for June.

Her thoughts slammed to a stop and she looked up to see Janice and Pax watching her with smug, benign little smiles.

Harmony frowned back at them. No, she would not kiss Jonah under the mistletoe ball.

No, she hadn't met her match as Pax was thinking; he was relishing her demise as his "unattached little sister." Janice was hoping for a really beautiful wedding.

Pax plotted to take Janice on a second honeymoon while Jonah helped Harmony with the ranch and children— Har-

mony blocked out her brother's thoughts about romancing his
"bride."

*So I want to lick expensive champagne from my wife's navel
without worrying about the kids waking up. So what?* Pax
asked belligerently as he glowered at her.

Harmony lifted her nose and looked away. She tossed back
a "last word." *Just don't count on me to take care of your
friend, Mr. Ho Ho.*

He's gotten to you. Pax's last amused thought caused Harmony to level a dark glare at her brother.

Then they sensed a third mental-chat-presence and looked at
Jonah. He was frowning as though something disturbed him.
He glanced at Pax, then at Harmony, and his rapid thoughts
flashed across hers. While Pax and Harmony transferred
smoothly paced thoughts, Jonah's were action packed. *Mr. Ho
Ho?*

Pax began to laugh outright, startling Janice who was snuggled against him. She worried if his painkillers were too high of
a dosage.

Shrimp was "girl-talking" with Pax's German shepherd,
Crystal. Shrimp envied Crystal's feminine name and deeply,
truly hated Motown music; she loved Western, which was more
cultural, in her opinion. She dreaded Jonah playing Motown
records to her later that night while they stayed in a motel.

Then Jimmy climbed up on Santa Claus's lap and began
chattering about raising rabbits with long, dangling ears. He'd
seen them at the state fair. Jonah listened intently and agreed
that Jimmy might get them in the spring, a Christmas rain-
check. When Linda, a busy three-year-old, climbed on Santa's
other knee, Jonah gathered her close. Sissy, at four years old,
wouldn't be left behind and the tall broad-shouldered Santa
Claus made room for her on his lap, too.

The children giggled and exclaimed and scampered from his
lap as he gave them all another gift.

Harmony breathed a relieved sigh. In a few moments,
"Santa" would leave to deliver presents to other children and
Jonah would "arrive," eat dinner and do his Western "git
along."

If he just didn't look so lonely at times. If only he didn't think of his daughter and mourn for her each time Sissy tilted her head.

Maybe he should stay with Pax's family, while Harmony trudged back to her snug little cabin. If he weren't in too much pain, Pax might be able to help Jonah sleep. He really needed the warmth of a family around him tonight. Motown records in a motel room just weren't enough on Christmas Eve.

"And what about you, little sweetheart?" Jonah-Santa was saying as he patted his knee.

Harmony straightened, the bells on her wrist jingling merrily, mocking her, as she touched the cupid on her chest. "Me?"

The children giggled and pulled her to her feet.

Jonah had her. He'd tossed out his lasso and snared her while she was thinking how he needed sleep—

"I'm a little old and a bit too large," she said with a forced smile.

"Never too old to sit on Santa's lap," Jonah stated with a deep "ho-ho. You'll fit just fine," he added.

No one ever challenged her; Harmony devoted her life to being very careful and avoiding potential risks. Jonah's eyes and his lap looked like huge "warning, danger zone" areas.

Chicken. Jonah's taunt slapped her.

He's right, Pax thought. *Cluck...cluck.*

Harmony flashed a dark look at her brother. *Lay off.*

She allowed the children to take her to Jonah's knee.

Janice sighed dreamily. *Such a beautiful couple.*

While holding her breath, Harmony's expression sent Janice—who was a nonplayer in this mental game—a brief, but firm message.... *Jonah and I are not...will not be a "couple." Ever.*

Then Jonah's big hands were at her waist, shaping it, finding her softness and easing her firmly to his hard lap. Harmony sat very straight, bracing herself away from Jonah. His blue eyes darkened as he looked at her lips, then slowly down her body. He traced the cranberry sweater dress from curve to curve and down to the slit that revealed her knee. He liked her knees, she discovered, easing the dress over her legs.

Jonah gathered her closer, despite her stealthy resistance.

He blocked out her cupid bushwhacking threat; she knew he was too busy thinking about how good she felt in his arms. He wished the pillow weren't strategically located because he really wanted her breasts against him.

Harmony breathed slightly, taking care not to lift her chest against the pillow.

Jonah's big hand smoothed her waist and the gentle rise of her hip leisurely. His other hand crossed her thighs to draw her closer. His hand stayed open on her thigh, a warm, firm possession.

Janice let out a dreamy "Ohhh..."

Jonah's eyes locked with Harmony's and that warning lift of the hair on the nape of her neck began.

Waves of his desire hit her, hot and fierce. She caught a scent of his after-shave, a lime base, and a headier scent that was his alone. His fingers tightened slightly.

She read his thoughts: he'd like to pay her back for dropping those tantalizing little kisses on him. He considered her a real hit-and-run artist and she wasn't running the next time she tried a move like that on him. Jonah mentally labeled her as a "dingy hit-and-run filly." He thought she needed "reins put on her." Then there was some obscure, damning remark about Lucky Halfpenny, the nice cowboy she'd met at the local Christmas party.

Harmony frowned. She distinctly remembered Lucky's appreciation for the cut of her dress. When she discarded his sensual thoughts, she found his excellent taste in clothing and his desire to become a fashion designer. Lucky loved women like a gourmet loved fine wine. One day he would find a lovely woman who understood him, and was just now in the sorting-through process.

"Tell Santa what you want for Christmas," Jonah was saying, holding her firmly despite her latest attempt to gracefully rise to her feet.

Without thinking, Harmony leaned close to his ear and whispered, "Let me go, you king-size Western cut of beef. Listen, buckaroo... if you have a brain in your head, you'll realize that if you behave now and let me go, I won't entirely destroy you."

Jonah's eyebrows shot up. The lines beside his eyes crinkled with laughter. She could feel it in him, tormenting her. "How?" he returned in a whisper.

"How what?"

"How are you going to destroy me?"

She leaned back and studied his cocky grin beneath the beard. She considered that in her past no one had challenged her wish to be free. She hadn't really used her powers to the maximum levels, but Jonah was pushing her to her limits.

While she was debating, Jonah acted suddenly. He stood up with her in his arms and walked to the hallway. While she dealt with being lifted easily and the flurry of excitement as the children leapt to follow them, Jonah said, "Have to go now. The other children are waiting."

He placed her on her feet beneath the mistletoe ball and hurried out of the house.

Then suddenly Pax needed the children to bring him another cup of cider and Janice hurried off to check the roasting turkey.

Harmony stood beneath the mistletoe ball and shook, the result of fighting anger she would not allow to escape.

Jonah was not making her angry. Or making her eat too much. She was just tired from getting her shop in working order and getting settled in the cabin. She could have a touch of flu and needed a soothing cup of herbal tea.

But Jonah—alias Mr. Ho Ho—was not getting to her.

When he returned any second now, she'd be firm, aloof, yet pleasant . . . keeping her Christmas cheer. With rules and a distance between them, she'd ask him how she could repay him for saving her life.

She didn't like owing that buckaroo anything.

Then Janice was sweeping by her and opening the door to Jonah. He stepped into the hallway and walked straight to Harmony. "I'm glad you stayed put. Didn't want to let my beard get in the way of this, little sweetheart," he murmured with a wicked, boyish grin that captivated her.

Pax and Janice were urging the children into the other room; Harmony was drawn against Jonah quickly, smoothly, firmly. The hallway light switched off; the shadows enclosed Jonah and herself. . . .

She had time to blink before Jonah's mouth settled down on hers.

She was floating amid a soft stream of seeking, tender, warm, hungry kisses. His lips tempted the corners of her lips, the upper curve, soothing her lower lip. She wasn't certain what he wanted, but she moved closer to the fire she sensed within him; her arms slid upward to his shoulders, seeking the safety there as her world slanted, shifted, and the kisses changed. Or had she changed them?

His hand cupped the back of her head, moving her lips up to him while his other arm gathered her close . . . so close that his heat warmed her body . . . so close that with little effort, she could move into him. . . .

Jonah's fingers were moving in her hair, gathering it, smoothing, caressing the weight. The span of his other hand slid along her back, molding her to him, urging her breasts against his body, following the shape of her back to her waist, then gently caressing the shape of her upper hip.

So sweet . . . wooing . . . courting. . . .

The crisp texture of his hair delighted her fingertips, the nape of his neck strong, warm beneath her touch.

Strength and heat lodged in the masculine contours of his cheeks, the line of his jaw.

The first tentative taste of his tongue surprised her; she caught him, drew him into her warmth, savoring him.

He breathed sharply, changing the angle of the kiss, deepening it, gathering her closer. She stood on tiptoe now, reaching for him, keeping him close. She disregarded the tinkling of the tiny bells on her wrist and gave herself to the warmth Jonah was creating within her.

One of them was shaking.

They both were.

Though her lids were closed, she saw the hallway's chandelier crystals set off a myriad of brilliant, colored lights. Only, the sparkling, shimmering beauty was pinging throughout her body and whirling around their heads. Or was it?

Jonah's hand slid lower, caressing her hips, shaping them, squeezing lightly.

She prowled through her reaction to his touch; she liked it. She loved the gentle claiming.

Harmony dug her fingers into Jonah's broad shoulders, enjoying the rippling cords, the padded muscles flexing as he moved against her.

She dived into him. Wallowed in him. Traced each masculine curve against her softness. He fit perfectly. His low, husky groan delighted her, and then his hips and thighs gently eased against her, his hands cupping, gathering her bottom into his palms as he moved her against him.

Desire. Heat. Storms and the incredible hunger.

Against her cheek, Jonah was breathing very unevenly. He began to tremble, his face hot against her throat as he stood very still, his body rigid. "You set me off," he stated raggedly.

Harmony blinked and swallowed, her body beginning to tremble as she realized that only Jonah's strong arms kept her from pooling to the floor. She felt as though a match had lit her dynamite, too—at least lit her fuse, she corrected. The actual dynamite was still waiting, aching for ignition....

"This is awful," she whispered, not shielding her desperation.

"Sure is," he agreed, nuzzling her hair and kissing her temple. "You've got a little vein right there that is thumping a mile a minute."

"Buckaroo, get your nose out of my hair and your lips off my skin," Harmony ordered shakily. Then she closed her eyes savoring the gentle caress of her breasts. Jonah's long fingers squeezed gently, possessively, around her. She realized that she was leaning against his hands and that she could step free at any time.

She had laminated him against the hallway wall! She had pinned the cowboy to the wall with the thrust of her aching body...tethered him with her locked arms. Jonah leaned down to brush a kiss across her trembling lips, instantly soothing her jumbled emotions. Another sweet kiss and the slow, firm stroking of her back eased the awful aching of her body and her uncertainty.

He was thinking that she was a strong woman and she would give as good as she got. She stood very still, concentrating on Jonah's thoughts until he frowned as if something disturbed him. He looked down at her warily.

"Don't be wearing any low-cut dresses around Lucky Halfpenny...unless you want to be cooking his breakfast the next morning. He's fast," Jonah said ominously, his fingertips cruising across her nipples to the outer perimeter of her breasts and then down to lock on the curve of her waist.

"And you're not?" Her fingers tightened into the taut muscles of his arms. Whatever had happened, whatever whirlwind had caught her and flung her intentions aside, her body and heart told her she wasn't finished with riding the tempest or Jonah.

The wrinkles beside Jonah's dark blue eyes deepened. "Never have been with ladies. If I were in the mood to buy, I'd circle the herd and pick a nice safe little lady without flaky ideas."

He eased her gently away and smoothed her hair. "You might want to step into the powder room and do something about those lips. You're wearing my brand," he whispered huskily before walking away from her.

Harmony stared after Jonah. She watched the arrogant tilt of his head, his broad shoulders tapering down to those lean hips and long legs doing their lanky cowboy-swagger thing toward the dinner table. She wanted to leap after him, tear into him and "bulldog"—bear him to the floor. She wanted to mind-fog him with what he could do with himself—like kiss a buffalo. "'Wearing my brand'," she muttered. "'Circle the herd...flaky ideas.'"

Jonah was not dictating her next actions. She had plans of her own. Like the wall behind her back. She needed to lean on it to keep from crumbling to the hallway carpeting.

She glanced up, damning the gaily decorated mistletoe ball and whatever Christmas cheer left her susceptible to Jonah and his kisses.

Five

———

"Summoning Jonah here proves his 'dingbat heifer' theory." Harmony stirred the spaghetti sauce, and studied the swirling green pepper, onions and herbs. She smoothed her loose sweater and flowing slacks, her best "burglar black" outfit. She always wore it when she was locked into a plan, and with Jonah's unpredictability, she needed every bit of good luck available. She sniffed the aromatic delicious scents and wished she would learn to mind her own business.

The first week of the New Year was a perfect time to observe her resolutions, keeping to the streamlined design she had chosen for her life. She'd circled her jumbled emotions—there was no reason for Jonah's kiss under the mistletoe ball to stir her. None at all. She'd placed her reaction to his kisses in neat boxes, reasoning out the upsetting Jonah events in her life. She'd been weak and woozy after those kisses because she'd been grabbed unexpectedly and because her breath had been whisked away. Lack of oxygen would make any woman's head spin and her knees weak.

Now, she was ready for Jonah. "I've never sent my thoughts into the wind to summon anyone before. It might not work and then I won't have to worry about Jonah. For today, anyway."

She owed Jonah a huge debt for saving her life in that blizzard. Of course Pax loved to underline that point repeatedly, and her honor decreed that she couldn't owe Jonah and watch him suffer. Nor would she be the victim of Pax's tormenting. She'd help ease Jonah into the reality that he possessed certain powers—and they were becoming stronger, despite his resistance. Once he realized his abilities, she'd be free of all obligations.

She pushed the bits of green pepper with her wooden spoon and wished Jonah Fargo—arrogant, moody, lone-wolf cowboy—hadn't kissed her. She wished she hadn't reached for him like a thirsty woman stranded on a hot, desert island reaches for a glass of ice lemonade. She flipped the image to a cold woman reaching for a warm coat and hot, mulled cider.

Harmony braced her hands on the worn, wooden counter of the old cabin and tried to concentrate on her new cupid weather-vane design. In copper it would be beautiful, gleaming in the sun and aging beautifully into rich tones. The huge room that was now her workshop was once a cowboy bunkroom. The lighting was perfect and the room's aura was friendly and creative. Pax had installed a wood pellet stove in her workroom and in the main room, her kitchen, dining and living room. A portable generator would serve in the winter if the electric lines snapped under ice and snow.

Her bedroom—an old saddle and bridle room—was just as appealing with her huge walnut carved four-poster bed and chest of drawers and heavy patchwork quilts. She studied the small patchwork quilt covering her dinner table.

If only Jonah hadn't said his goodbyes on Christmas Eve with a grim determination that holiday loneliness suited him.

If only he hadn't kissed her under the mistletoe ball and complicated everything, she could—

No, she did not feel sorry for him.

Well...yes, she did. Trust good old Harmony to want to rescue a down-and-out, rangy, June-hungry, lip-sucking cowboy. Even as Jonah said his goodbyes that evening, Harmony could feel the shadows surging to enclose him. Her resolutions to leave Mr. Ho Ho alone had slanted immediately. No Motown tapes in a lonely motel room would take away his desperation or the sounds that plagued him. She'd caught herself taking a step to place her hands on his face, to warm him a bit for Christmas Eve.

But then, he probably dropped in to visit June for that little chore.

After her marriage, she'd learned that Mark had a woman friend. While his fear of Harmony kept his performance from peaking, his affair apparently satisfied him and made him feel like a superstud.

Harmony grabbed the dishcloth and scrubbed away a flour speck on her counter. She continued to scrub it thoroughly after the countertop was clean.

She concentrated on why she had summoned Jonah. She'd want to help anyone who was fighting his abilities and facing the mental echoes of his daughter crying for her doll.

When Jonah arrived, Harmony would be clinical, friendly, yet firm.

Why had she summoned him? Why had she stood in the wind, focused on her cupid wind chimes and called him to her?

Harmony studied the bells on her wrist. Somehow, Jonah could disengage her alarm systems. He also had enough powers to make her mind go blank while he was kissing her.

She'd promised herself that the next man who kissed her would be harmonious, understanding, kind, sharing and all the rest, she thought impatiently. Jonah did not fit her prespecifications or even the mold for a dinner date. She sniffed the spaghetti sauce, added a dash of chili powder, a pinch of oregano, and corrected her thoughts. This was mental telepathy business. ESP business . . . not man-woman business. She was involved because . . . because she did owe him a major debt and she wouldn't be free until she repaid him.

She tapped her fingers on the counter and inhaled the scent of freshly baked breadsticks. Jonah could prick her temper with one scowl. He had "bristling yard dog" written all over his harsh features.

Harmony shifted her weight restlessly and placed her fingers on the tiny bells. She was very careful now, expressing herself in different ways without the use of words such as *aura, reading* and *seeing.* She'd conditioned herself to use caution, using her abilities very carefully and as a last resort.

If ever a human needed a last resort—a showdown effort—
it was Jonah Fargo. Harmony hoped that she could pry his
mental bricks aside and open the wall for Jonah to appreciate
his abilities.

That was why she had stood in the freezing wind and tossed
her thoughts to Jonah, like notes in an ocean-bound bottle.
Because she cared and knew the pain he was experiencing.

Without the presence of Janice, Pax and the children, Harmony intended to give Jonah a demonstration of his powers.
One he couldn't deny.

She'd feed him and fog him and then she'd step back into the
smooth-flowing groove she had chosen for her life-style. She'd
maintain a mentoring, benign attitude throughout his learning
process. She patted her hair, which she had pulled high on top
of her head to appear more businesslike, and listened to the
jingling bells. Temper and wild emotions did not suit her, not
at all. Once Jonah was properly fogged and beginning to understand, he could borrow her books on documented paranormal experience and exploring the realms within. She'd give him
a few hard-earned tips about adjustment to an abnormal
power, then she'd ease away.

Jonah stopped running in his snowshoes, pausing to study
the old cabin and the smoke coming from the chimney. He adjusted his ski mask against the freezing wind and resented his
need to see Harmony, to talk with her. Four o'clock in the afternoon of an icy day was not the time to drop in on neighbors. He should be holed up with Shrimp, who refused to leave
her warm blanket. Lately Shrimp had been thinking that she
needed emotional distance from Jonah. If she needed to be let
out, she would use the trapdoor he had installed in the back
porch.

The icy wind cut through the small cloud of his breath and
he shook his head. "As long as I'm this close, I might as well
check on the mind reader for Pax."

He probably wasn't the only cowboy roaming in the vicinity
of Harmony's house. Lucky was foaming at the mouth, waiting for Harmony to come into town. Joe Moon had plans for
"the new lady in town," and men of all ages were hounding
Pax, inquiring about his little sister. Once they discovered she

was single, it was like throwing bait to hungry coyotes, Jonah
thought as he shuffled his snowshoes toward the cabin. If she
sprang that mind-reading swami stuff on them, they'd be
emotionally damaged for life. As her rescuer and Pax's friend,
Jonah was duly obliged to protect her against the pack of
bachelors . . . and them against her weird ideas. The next thing
the Fort Benton bachelors knew, they'd be sitting around a
candlelit table, holding hands and listening for voices of the
dearly departed.

Then there was her backside. Summer was coming, and
without her bulky winter coat, Harmony's round backside
would be swaying and causing traffic jams on the one main
street. Harmony's hot-furnace kisses would probably damage
Randy Phillips's heart beyond repair. Remembering her sweet,
soft, hungry lips certainly hadn't helped Jonah relax. Between
listening to the crying, Shrimp understanding his commands
before he spoke them aloud, dishes bashing against the wall and
the memory of Harmony's soft full body in his arms, Jonah
wasn't sleeping at all.

Fear of being bashed by a herd of cupids kept him awake. He
tensed, realizing right now, within hearing distance of Harmony's wind chimes, that he feared those cupids more than her
psychic hogwash.

Any way he looked at the Harmony Davis situation, she
presented a picture of disaster. She set him off. Rather than
tangle with Harmony's off-center ideas, he'd rather face a—

Harmony opened the door before he knocked; she'd probably seen him coming. "Come in," she said, drawing him into
the house.

Jonah blinked. Harmony hadn't spoken or moved. She was
looking at him with those huge soft wheat-gold eyes and he
ached to move into her arms. Her lips moved as she said aloud,
"Supper is waiting. I've been expecting you, Jonah. I hope you
like spaghetti."

"I like spaghetti," he said, glancing at the table set for two,
and inhaling the scent of fresh bread. "I like breadsticks and
freshly made pasta, too."

He studied her hair, piled on top of her head and the hoops
in her ears. The bells on Harmony's wrist jingled as she lifted
one hand to smooth back a curl while he watched with interest

and noted the trembling of her fingers. He remembered them
fluttering across his shoulders when they kissed.

No kissing this time, Jonah, a tiny, firm, feminine voice
warned him.

"Good. I'm glad you like spaghetti and breadsticks," she
murmured, taking his coat, ski mask and hat from him and
hanging them on a brass clothes rack. She turned to face him,
one hand gripping the bells on her other wrist. They tinkled
slightly and her fingers tightened over them. "Just how did you
know I baked breadsticks, Jonah? The frozen ones are quite
good and much easier. The 'freshly made pasta' is from my
machine."

"The pasta machine is on the counter and I recognized the
smell of spaghetti...garlic." He shrugged, recognizing her I've-
got-you tone. She didn't have him. Harmony wasn't an easy-to-
do-anything lady. If she decided to go for something, she'd pay
attention to every detail. Right now, he had the notion that one
of her major details and problems was himself. Since her kisses,
the vision of a mole on her left breast and a strawberry birthmark on her right buttock had been moving through his nights
and days, she deserved to pay. Harmony Davis was a woman
locked onto a mission, and while he was curious, he wasn't
making anything easy for her. "Pasta goes with spaghetti sauce.
So does red wine. Maybe a cabernet sauvignon."

"Yes, red wine is great with spaghetti. Isn't it interesting that
I do have a bottle of cabernet sauvignon ready for an early
dinner?" she asked lightly, moving toward the stove. She removed a basket of breadsticks and placed them on the table
beside the pasta and the spaghetti sauce. He recognized her
smooth, I-have-this-planned movements. "Shall we eat?"

Marching to Harmony's tune wasn't on his agenda, Jonah
decided as he glanced around the old cabin. "Where's your
crystal ball?" he asked, noting the potted herbs on the win-
dowsill and the comfortable warmth of her home. "You've got
a baby quilt on your dinner table."

"I know. It's a current cottage decor thing. My crystal ball
is still packed. If you'd like to look around before we eat,
please ... be my guest," Harmony offered in a too-polite tone
and a tight smile as she cast a meaningful glance at the waiting
dinner.

"Thank you," Jonah returned, recognizing the tiny ping of satisfaction zipping through him; he'd gotten to her. He enjoyed ruffling her control. He inhaled the various fragrances of her home—a drift of cinnamon and that distinctive, fresh wildflower scent with just a nip of exotic heat. Afghans, quilts, braided rugs, a stash of dried flowers here and hanging herbs there... The room was very neat, feminine, comfortable and lacking in a man's touch. No man would sit his bottom on that bouquet of flowers serving as her couch.

"Where are your tarot cards?" he asked while considering her bookshelves. She was a very neat lady, the books arranged according to subject. Psychic phenomena books spread across three shelves. Another shelf was devoted to discovering herself as a woman, feminine empowerment, retaining personality essences and relationships. There were two shelves of metalworking and one of how-to's and home remedies.

She inhaled sharply and Jonah wandered into her workroom, flipping on the bald overhead lights. A calendar of things to do per hour of the day, per day of the month was listed; neat check marks placed opposite each task. Sheets of copper and brass hung from pegs, a neat arrangement of catalogs and tools lay in a precise line on her worktable. Bottles of chemicals stood in a big-to-small, labeled row on a wall shelf. Gloves, welding goggles, torch and lighter, were all very neatly aligned next to a huge, unfinished, copper cupid weather vane.

Jonah touched the metal lightly, reminded of the night the cupids jumped him and he'd envisioned Harmony in her black nightie.

One of his New Year's resolutions had been to stay away from her vicinity, yet here he was, prowling through her nest as though he were trying it on for size.

I owe you my life, buckaroo. I'm going to repay you and then you can just vamoose.

Jonah tightened his hand on a reel of copper wire. *Leave it,* he shot back to the empty workshop.

What? And owe you? Not on your life!

Jonah turned very carefully to Harmony who was standing in the door to the living room. Her loose sweater and flowing slacks belonged around feed sacks—

I don't particularly care for your fashion sense or your comments on my attire. I invited you here to discuss your powers. I have decided to become your mentor.

Jonah reeled with rapid, angry, precise thoughts. He refused to rub his aching temples and gripped the workbench instead. "Jonah?" Harmony's soft voice slid through the echoes in his mind.

"Jonah, come to supper," she said gently as though she invited him to meals every day. She flipped off the light switch and waited for him, outlined in the light of the living room.

When he didn't move, trapped in a torrent of thoughts and some of them not his own, Harmony hurried toward him. She'd invited him? How?

In the shadows, her eyes were huge in her pale face, anxious for him. Her fingers were light, hypnotically warm on his temples, and the bells tinkled close to his ears....

He was kissing her then, gathering her close to him.

But Harmony's worried expression continued to peer up at him, her fingers making small circles on his throbbing temples.

Jonah shook his head slightly and closed his eyes. He wasn't holding her. He wasn't kissing her.

"Jonah," Harmony whispered softly aloud. "You aren't really kissing me. You're just thinking—mmmf," she said, her words interrupted by Jonah's mental kiss.

If this is in my mind, I may as well go to the end of the trail, he thought. He saw himself picking her up without breaking the kiss and carrying her into the bedroom.

He saw Harmony clinging to him, her lips moving warmly beneath his. He thought he heard her whisper a protest. *Jonah... I'm heavy. Put me down.*

But he didn't, because she was clinging too hard to him, her mouth parted, waiting for his kiss. She had a good strong feel to her, as if she would last out the bad times. He gathered her closer and said, "You're sweeter than the sunrise coming over the mountains. Sweeter than the morning dew on the clover."

"You are not holding me—carrying me," she corrected unevenly. "We're actually standing in my workshop."

"Am I kissing you?" he asked, closing his eyes and seeing himself brush his lips against hers, tasting her mouth with the tip of his tongue.

"Noo..." she returned breathlessly, her head tilting back as the image of him bending to kiss the line of her throat entered her mind. "Not really. You aren't touching me . . . really."

"Are you holding me close and tight? Is that your heart racing against me, or is it some sweet little butterfly aching to be free?"

Her hand was on his heart, sliding beneath his shirt to rest over his skin. "I . . . uh . . ."

"I want you, Harmony," he admitted shakily. "But I don't know where I am . . . what is happening to me."

"I know," she said with a sigh, moving her face into the shelter of his throat and shoulder. She stroked his chest with one hand and smoothed the taut nape of his neck with the other.

Jonah arched against the light, timid touch. She wasn't used to touching men. She was frightened of getting close to him; she sensed he would want too much. She was right.

Do you want me? he asked, fearing that she didn't. That she could destroy him with one word of reality. She was too precious to him now, too close, too sweet, too warm.

I can't. I'm a person who has to plan the events in my life. I haven't planned for this to happen and you don't fit my pre-specifications.

Afraid? He bit her earlobe gently, then kissed it. *I understand. Wanting . . . loving is a fearful thing. Are we talking aloud now or just thinking?*

Thinking. But. . . . She trembled in his arms; she didn't want to think about the "buts" and "ifs", reality and nonreality. *Take me to bed, Jonah. Love me.*

Is this real? he asked as he envisioned lowering her to the bed. *Real enough.*

He lay beside her, watching her, and realizing that he was caught in a daydream he didn't want to leave. *It's been a long time, sweetheart.*

You won't hurt me, Jonah, she thought, unbuttoning his shirt.

I want you to know that there is a caring here . . . now.

I know, she returned with a touch of sadness.

* * *

He'd want everything. She was frightened, Harmony thought as Jonah carefully lifted away her sweater in their shared fantasy.

She stood in the workshop, her feet firmly planted on the wooden boards and knew that she wanted to be with Jonah in the bedroom. She opened her mind to Jonah's, reveling in his pleasure, feeding on his delight and her own.

She swallowed, watching desire darken his eyes as he looked at her. He bent to kiss her chin, her throat, then lifted her hand to kiss the center of her palm. He slid his hand against hers, studying the light and dark blend of their skins, the different textures. "You are a fierce, strong woman, Harmony Davis. I fear that I shall be tested to my very limits."

She began to tremble, cold where he was not touching her. His eyes told her that she'd never been made love to like he wanted to love her. He wanted to fold her into him, to drink the sweetness from her lips and treasure her from head to toe. He wanted to hold her fine backside in his palms and he wanted her breasts etching sensual, rhythmic trails upon his skin while they made love. He wanted to drink from her lips a taste sweeter than wine and he wanted to—

Harmony gasped at Jonah's thoughts as they moved down her body. "Are you all talk?" she asked unevenly.

Jonah's slow grin disarmed and enchanted her. "How do you call it?" he asked, using the Western term that meant she could choose what she wanted. She knew that she had to have him that minute—that she must complete the sensual vision they'd both begun.

Now, she answered, her skin dampening with the need of him, her body heating and waiting.

I'm mighty glad you said that, he said, bending to kiss her breasts. *You are one fine woman. I am honored that you have decided to let me treasure you.*

Harmony shivered, ignored her warning bells, and whisked away their clothing. *I am also a woman of action, Jonah. Remember that.*

I truly will. Lying naked beside her, Jonah was magnificent as he tenderly kissed her hot cheek. *You've never seen a man in the all-together. Shyness becomes you, rosebud.*

It was her turn to say, *I'm mighty glad you said that,* as Jonah moved over her. For just that heartbeat, Mark's demeaning remarks lashed at her. Then Jonah settled firmly upon her, cherishing each curve, each feminine nuance, and she was "mighty glad."

Shall we? he asked, waiting for her with a tender smile. He was trembling now, keeping his weight and fierce desire from her.

Harmony reached and took what he would keep from her. When she drew his lips to her breast, she gasped with pleasure and with Jonah's thoughts that she tasted like a perfect little rosebud, unfolding her secrets to him.

This is making love... this is lovemaking, she thought as he filled her slowly, firmly, gently. Her fingers caught his shoulders, latching to the firm contours like an anchor, because she knew what was to come. She knew that whatever she had experienced before paled when compared to this... to Jonah.

Ready, rosebud? he asked tenderly, smoothing her damp cheek with trembling hands. *Am I hurting you?*

I... you... Jonah's hands found her bottom, lifting her higher, demanding everything, yet he was so gentle. She was complete now, here with him, and yet ached for more.

They were in the fire now, waiting, resting a bit before going on into the flames.

His eyes were closed now, a fine film of perspiration covering his face and gleaming on his shoulders as he concentrated on the warm fit of her locked tightly around him.

Harmony knew they were actually standing in her workshop. She could step away easily—

Then she, who planned her life, choosing her next step carefully, flung all her thoughts at him, eager for lovemaking, aching with unbearable pressure for this bond, this mating, this man making love to her in the flame....

Rosebud.... he whispered desperately against her throat, catching her close to him, anchoring her as the bond deepened and took flight.

Jonah's strength met her own, his hungers fueled upon hers and she wanted... wanted... wanted.... Then Jonah's hand slid between them, seeking, touching and she shattered, burst, flamed.

What did you do? she managed unevenly when he finally rested his forehead upon her shoulder, his lips brushing the racing pulse in her throat.

Why was he chuckling? Why was he filled with such joy, such freedom, and feeling like a boy? Jonah wondered before he allowed her to soothe him, drawing him down to sleep upon her soft, soft sweet rosebud breasts. He kissed them leisurely, his hand stroking her hips. Soft...satiny...pale...his sweet rosebud lady.

He gave himself to her care and wondered sleepily when he had trusted. He nuzzled her breasts, kissing the tips again and savoring the beat of her heart beneath his head. He shifted slightly, easing his weight to the side when she stirred restlessly, unwilling to leave her. When he kissed her cheek, he found a tear. *Don't cry, rosebud. Everything will work out fine, you'll see.*

Fine? she whispered unevenly, her blush enticing him. *Just fine?*

Then he looked at her and he knew that the flames weren't finished. *Be gentle with me, rosebud. That's a fierce look you're wearing,* he said as she moved over him.

You're going to pay for whatever you did a moment ago, she threatened as he treasured her breasts, molding them with caresses and tasting them again. He began to nibble gently and tenderly, aroused cords tightened, leading straight down to the very nest Jonah now resided in. She flexed her feminine muscles to show him that he should not test her goodwill. Harmony was not a woman to tamper with, this he would discover.

Are you all talk? he asked in a sexy challenge no woman could ignore.

Oh, right. Jonah falls into a dead sleep after mental lovemaking, Harmony thought, and she's left to deal with the aftermath and her nervous eating habit. She nestled in the couch, drew the quilt to her chin and stared at the flames in her pellet stove and tried not to think about the fully dressed, sleeping man on her bed.

The pile of books discarded to her floor had not divulged enormous amounts about mental, earth-shaking, sensual fulfillment while standing fully clothed in a cold room. She frowned at the closed door to her shop. There they had stood amid her torches and burnishing pads, making very warm love while neither of them moved.

Right. She, Harmony Davis, an extremely cautious psychic and should-know-better divorcée, had just flung herself at Jonah and taken him to his delight. And hers. She'd fogged him with lovemaking, flinging herself at him and loving every minute.

He hadn't been with June; she knew that instinctively. Another woman's touch wasn't riding on his skin . . . that marvelous tanned skin flowing over hard cords and muscles.

Harmony nibbled on her Jonah problem, lying asleep in the bedroom, and the cold breadstick; she'd already eaten three. She tapped her fingers on the quilt's embroidered rosebuds, then gingerly lifted her hand away. "Rosebud." She repeated his endearment. He made her sound as though she were fresh and sweet and delicate.

Her hand trembled when she shoved back a heavy swathe of curls. She wasn't delicate or new or . . . what was that Jonah thought? "Soft as a baby rabbit's belly."

Transferring Jonah's body from her shop into her bed was a giant maneuver. He'd leaned heavily upon her and it had taken all of her strength—and that was depleted—to urge him into the bedroom. He was deeply asleep before his head touched the pillow. He hungered sleepily for her breasts. He'd snuggled into the pillow with a Cheshire cat smile and murmured, "Rosebuds."

Harmony curled her legs tighter beneath her and pressed the quilt to her aching breasts. Her body was extremely sensitive now, thank you very much to Mr. Fargo.

He'd looked so worn, shadows around his eyes, his cheeks gaunt. One look at him and she'd known he was fighting for control, that the crying hadn't stopped. When he'd gripped the workbench and paled, her damnable caring instincts went into overdrive and she'd opened herself to him.

She scowled at the cold spaghetti sauce and wine, which had had too much time to "breathe." Mark never caused her this much tension or trembling or pure fear. He'd never held her as tightly and safely, as though nothing could separate them and he would fight to keep her near. While Mark glanced at the bedside clock to time his lovemaking, Jonah had concentrated on making love to her. But then, once Mark had discovered her powers, he'd always been a little afraid—

She had not mated... bonded with Jonah. Nothing had happened... actually happened... really happened.

Harmony glanced at the candle and pushed away the image of a man and woman making passionate love inside the flames. She squirmed upon the flower bouquet upholstery. She wasn't certain that she could handle real lovemaking with Jonah. In reality, he'd be even more demanding, more hungry, bigger... sweeter... more delicious....

"'How do you call it?'" she muttered, reaching for another breadstick and crushing it in her fingers when the bed creaked with Jonah's restless movements.

How did she call it? She'd reached and grabbed and loved Jonah without holding back. She closed her eyes, tapping into his dreams, and found him making love to her again, this time very gentle, very sleepy, dreamy, beautiful lovemaking.

"Oh, Jonah," she whispered in a sigh as she sensed his power filling her.

Come here, hungry lady, he ordered in a sleepy, sexy thought.

"Shh. Go back to sleep."

This is where you belong. He cradled her against him, smoothing her hip and placing his hand over her breast. He was sleeping even as he eased his thigh over hers. He sighed deeply, like a man who has known great pleasure and who reluctantly admitted the need to rest before beginning again.

Again? Jonah was sleeping deeply now in her bedroom, and Harmony locked her fingers onto the couch's arm. She'd been netted twice, or rather she had actively participated, doing her share of the netting. She wasn't actually the nettee, if she admitted the truth. Jonah hadn't made her do anything that she didn't desperately want to do... with him.

Harmony straightened with the awareness that she'd never wanted Mark so intensely. She'd never wanted him to the height that she had desired Jonah.

The stirring of her passion hovered restlessly within her body, demanding that she really go into the bedroom . . . that she really snuggle close to Jonah and let him cuddle her in his sleep.

He was a really good cuddler. Of course, she hadn't been cuddled and treasured and cherished and made love to like Jonah had just done in his mind.

Harmony blinked, remembering the height of their passion, and Jonah's desperate thought to control himself and not to frighten her...this time. Because the next time he got a hold of her, he was showing her how a woman should be loved with no holding back, no-holds-barred, and nothing between. She wouldn't get by with this fast little flurry that had exhausted him so much.

There was more to Jonah's lovemaking? Harmony wondered incredulously, her body tensing.

It didn't matter. They hadn't made love actually; layers of clothing had stayed between them. They hadn't shared a bed; they had stood upright in her workshop without touching each other. She refused to believe she'd acted out of instinct and that she had . . . Harmony swallowed deeply and closed her eyes. *Whatever had happened, she refused to believe that she had bonded with Jonah Fargo.*

Nor had she substituted for June Fields, the vamp. Jonah was far too intense to be transferring his needs.

She tapped her fingers on the upholstery's tiny rosebuds, then jerked her hand away. She'd find a different way to repay Jonah for saving her life, because getting close to him was too dangerous.

Jonah was not predictable fodder for a mentoring program.

Six

———

Jonah raised his hand to knock on Harmony's welding helmet, then lowered it. The ten o'clock sun coming through the old wavery glass windows skimmed down Harmony's body. Every curve was outlined in sunlight, her braids thick and gleaming. He curled his fingers into a fist and tried not to glance at the skin-tight spandex covering her backside.

He inhaled sharply, remembering the curve of each round shape filling his palms, the muscles moving beneath her skin. He locked his fingers into his thigh to keep them from reaching for her—

Emotions had run between them, laying tender on his mind. Sweet, caring looks, soft touches, seeking hunger.... He distinctly remembered doing some welding of his own with Harmony, the deep-down kind—making her a part of him, of his heart and life. In his dream—because that was what his weird memories had to be—no blowtorch could have cut them apart. They would have just flowed back together like a river, separated then rejoined on their path to that final, stunning, starburst moment.

But then a man couldn't do personal welding in his sleep, in his dreams or while he had every stitch of his clothes on, could

he? His jeans and sweater and shirt were wrinkled from sleep.
He must have pulled his boots off sometime in the night. They
were on his feet now and he was standing fully dressed, watching Harmony attack a metal monster. *This* was reality, not
glimpses of heat and tenderness, movement and her tears.

Tears? Jonah's frown deepened, triggering the headache that
had been plaguing him since he awoke smothered in lacy pillowcases and flowery sheets. When he dreamed about a woman
crying after making love with him, he'd really stepped over the
edge.

Harmony continued to weld, her blowtorch hissing, as she
bent, angling her helmet to work on the grotesque, huge crea-
ture she was creating in a corner of her workshop. The clump-
clump of her highly laced, workman's boots echoed in the
workshop as she moved around the grotesque metal piece,
stabbing away impatiently with her torch until the metal
glowed. She worked like a knight fighting a dragon...or woman
with a burr under her saddle.

Her braids seemed to leap around her shoulders with a life of
their own, glistening in the sunlight. The tiny little chest-
hugging spandex top she wore looked as if it were bursting at
the seams.

Jonah closed his eyes and swallowed. He remembered
something about bursting at his seams, but this morning,
physical evidence didn't support his memories.

He inhaled, stepped close to her and knocked on her helmet. He'd leave as soon as he thanked her for letting him—
what? Spend the night? Sleep in her bed? Love her in his
dreams?

Just then, Harmony straightened, turned off her blowtorch
and placed it on the workbench. She turned slowly to Jonah
and raised the safety shield of her helmet. Her expression was
guarded and Jonah mourned the tiny satisfied smile he'd
dreamed on her lips. "Good morning," she said very carefully
in an aloof tone. "I hope you slept well."

"'Morning. I'll be on my way now. I appreciated the bed."

"You needed rest. I'm glad you were able to sleep."

Jonah ran his hand through his hair, then down his unshaven jaw. "I can't remember leaving the workshop and
walking to your bed. I apologize for spending the night. I

haven't been sleeping well.... I guess it caught up with me. Sorry."

She removed her helmet and stripped away the huge welder's gloves. She reached for a man's large flannel shirt, slid her arms into and buttoned it very quickly. "I'm glad I could help."

He didn't intend to take her braid out of the shirt and lay it carefully on her shoulder. She shivered when he touched her, his fingers lingering on the warm, thickly woven hair. It was like her: strong, solid, smooth to the touch and bearing her feminine scent. But then she stood there with one tawny-reddish braid under the shirt and the other out . . . he felt duty-bound to ease the trapped braid free, too. Harmony looked sweet and shy as she looked down at the floor and shivered . . . just once.

Jonah forced his hand away. His muscles tensed, his heart lurched, and his stomach flip-flopped as a slow blush rose up her cheeks. He felt light-headed, like a groom after his wedding night. Like a man who knew that his chosen woman was all-woman, sweet and shy and delicate and very responsive, very shocked and greedy, and caring. His body felt sated, yet hungry for her warmth, her fire. And her mouth. His mind was really slanting, because he wanted to gather her to him and share his heart with her.

But Harmony's dark gold eyes were clear and too bright as she looked up at him; her body was too rigid. The angles of her eyebrows and cheekbones were sharp now, not merging with the softness of her rosebud lips as they had in his dream.

"I was just checking on you for Pax. I suppose your nose is out of joint because I took your only bed last night," he said, lunging into the safety of a thrust, rather than standing there longing to take her into his arms and kiss her hot cheeks and tell her how sweet she was in his dream.

"I am no such thing. You needed sleep and I was only too glad to sleep on my couch. After all, you shared your home with me." Her blush deepened and the tiny vein along her temple raced.

"People will talk about you and me now," he commented, glancing at the willful tendrils catching the sunlight like a halo around her head. While he wasn't particularly fond of her off-center thinking, he didn't want gossip hurting her. His body ached for hers, to fold her close to him and protect her and cuddle her. A fierce, proud woman with dingbat ideas wouldn't like that. But she had—in his dream. She'd purred and cuddled, and that tiny bit of a surprised, muffled scream had really pleased him. Because she had been so surprised, so hungry in his dream, Jonah remembered straining to hold back—because he didn't want to frighten her that first time. At the end of the dream, he remembered promising himself that the next time they made love, he would not hold anything back from his sweet little rosebud.

Harmony frowned slightly and stepped back, her work boots clumping on the wood floor. Her hand fluttered to close the shirt collar; her knuckles paled as she gripped it tightly. "I doubt that there will be gossip. You're not the sort of man who I would encourage to spend the night."

They were locked in battle now, like fencers with foils, jabbing, keeping their defenses. Jonah mourned his dream and folded it away. "Good enough. I'll leave now. I just wanted to thank you before I left."

She nodded stiffly and gripped the horn of her metal monster. She smoothed it with a lover's fingers, and Jonah's body tightened into a hard knot. Since he was riding a morning-after-the-loving without his dream bride, it didn't take much to stir him.

"You're welcome," she murmured.

He didn't fit her prespecifications. She liked easy, comfortable men—men who were predictable and relationship moldable. The angry, jumbled thoughts flashed through Jonah's mind—something about the impossibility of bonding and mating. Jonah stared at her and realized that every muscle in his body had tensed, resenting Harmony's bonding and mating ideas. While his body felt as though he'd spent the night making love to her—and that was just a dream—he sure didn't have a sweetheart-bride this morning.

She didn't fit his idea of a comfortable woman, either. No righteous woman would caress that nightmarish metal dragon's horn in front of a man who ached in his every fiber to have her. His throat tightened and he shifted restlessly, uncomfortable with the burgeoning tight knot heating his body.

"Are you going to bulldog that thing?" he asked hoarsely as her fingers circled the metal horn.

You tell me, Mr. Ho Ho. Then Harmony carefully uncurled her fingers from the metal and Jonah's body lurched precariously.

He was not sweating, he thought as she frowned curiously at his upper lip. And if he was, the workshop was overheated.

They looked at each other, not giving an inch. He knew then that Harmony did not recognize what a sensual touch could do to a man, and a little happy cloud filled him.

Reacting to the nonsense in his mind, he smote that unexplainable cheeriness and killed it.

"You stay on your side of the street, and I'll stay on mine," Jonah stated slowly, nettled unexpectedly when he thought of other men touching Harmony, kissing that mobile, soft mouth. No telling what big ideas the area's unmarried men would have in the bonding and mating department. Since they didn't share his immunity to her, they might go off the deep end the first time they saw her do her welding dance in that tight getup and braids.

Happy little golden clouds weren't on his menu de life.

"Any man interested in you has my sympathy," he said aloud and stripped away the emotion he was feeling just then. Jealousy had never fitted him.

"You can't tell me what side of the street to walk on," she returned evenly, her eyes narrowing and sunlight raining sparks on her hair.

"I could tell you plenty. Like you'd better keep your crazy ideas to yourself." Who needed a woman wearing braids, spandex and heavy workman's boots anyway? He glanced at the metal horn and breathed deeply, relieving himself of the last remnants of his uncomfortable moment.

"You...are...a...closed-minded dinosaur. Why I ever...?" she began hotly. Her eyes widened slightly and her lips pressed shut.

"Ever what?" Jonah shot back, his hunting instincts leaping to life and focusing on her. What had she done? What secrets flickered behind those furious tiger eyes and arched brows?

Because the tight set of her lips said she wouldn't answer him, he asked the question that had been pricking him. He glanced at the huge, curved, bristling metal affair. "What's that thing you were attacking in the corner?"

"I call it 'Therapy.' You may leave now," she offered in a soft, imperial tone.

"One more question, little sweetheart. Whose shirt are you wearing?" Why should he care? Why was it so important?

"Mine, of course." Her boot clump-clumped impatiently. Most women tapped their toes, Jonah thought. But the woman of his dreams—not Harmony. The woman who stood there— the woman stirring him up and making him feel like a bride- groom without his bride, and setting him off—wore heavy "steel-toed" workboots. She lifted her head defiantly. "As I said, you may leave."

The flash of her eyes told him he'd gotten to her. He al- lowed the pleasure to fill him and left her with a smirk. He knew the shirt was Pax's—he dismissed her ideas that he had "powers." He must have seen Pax wearing it, because the shirt belonged to her brother. Harmony had kept her life very un- cluttered with personal relationships and that meant men didn't come close to her and love her and leave their shirts in her house.

For him, there wouldn't be any loving Harmony Davis. He knew better than to ask for more trouble in his life. He was not asking her any more questions, and he hadn't made love to her, and he didn't want to know anything at all about bonding and mating—

"Jonah?" Her soft voice caught him as he stood in the doorway.

When he turned slowly to her, his heart ached as though he were leaving a part of himself with her. His instincts told him that he wouldn't heal easily...that he'd remember the sight of her standing in that huge shirt, her legs sheathed in spandex, and her boots...he'd remember her braids flowing like red- dish gold ropes down her chest as she caught her bracelet. The muffled sounds of bells died eerily in the wall of dusty sun- light between Jonah and the woman he unaccountably ached to hold.

"Take care of yourself, Jonah," Harmony said quietly as if she were saying goodbye forever.

Goodbye forever suited him fine, he thought grimly as he closed the door. If he were losing his mind, he could do it by himself—without Harmony setting him off and that bonding and mating nonsense echoing in his brain.

Then why did he hurt so much, as if he were leaving a part of his heart with her?

Isolation suited Jonah; loneliness stretched out on the snow-covered wheat fields beside the road. Without other people nearby, he was alone with his thoughts. Almost three months had passed since he'd trekked to Harmony's and spent the night under her roof. Now he was driving home to Fargo land, after working as a hired man for other ranchers.

He rubbed his new mustache, a whimsical adventure, since he'd never had one. He liked the feeling of controlling something in his life, even if it was only trimming his mustache.

With March flying out the door, Jonah still wondered why that morning at Harmony's he felt like a lover without his morning-after kiss. He understood his need to check on her; she was Pax's sister and Pax's broken leg needed rest. As a neighbor, Jonah always did his part. And he'd been tired, stretched to the limits with his faulty mind, so he'd badly needed sleep when he arrived on her doorstep.

If he could just find a reasonable—or unreasonable explanation—why the first time he saw her backside, he wanted to fill both palms with her and turn her for his hungry kiss.

He wasn't a kissing man...not counting the time she'd moved into his arms and kissed him first. That was the evening he'd dreamed that the cupids had bushwhacked him.

Days of exhausting ranch work and nights of repairing farm machinery couldn't rip away that dream, or the sound of the child crying.

Jonah inhaled sharply, ignoring the hollow feeling within his heart.

Okay. A reasonable explanation might be that a man didn't wake up every morning to a woman welding "Therapy" and clumping in work boots.

The image of Harmony standing in her snug house, her braids glistening in the sunlight and her legs sheathed in spandex, didn't leave Jonah very much think room.

Every time he lit a welding torch to repair metal, he saw Harmony clumping, attacking her project. She had a memorable backside and the sunlight had seemed to glow around her.

Once the welding memory snagged him, he was a goner, going right off over the edge and thinking about making dream-love to her.

Jonah scanned the snow melting under the late-March sun and tightened his gloved hands around the steering wheel. Fort Benton country was as it had always been—before the Blackfoot, the fur traders, before the Fargos. Spring wheat would be sprouting soon, fed by the snow's moisture. The cattails would be growing in the buffalo wallows, and the berry bushes would begin to leaf. When he could, he'd drive into town and collect the new sheet-metal roofing he'd ordered. Hard work, not silly night-after-the-honeymoon hungers, would keep him occupied.

Making dream-love to Harmony could really tilt a man's sanity.

Mule deer and antelope would be taking their young across the fields to water near the coulees filled with willows.

Cupids and jingle bells and telepathy and an aging cowboy's sensual needs and fantasies were a bad mix. Toss in the child's crying in his mind and his full deck was missing a few cards.

Jonah ruffled Shrimp's fur, then slid his hand to rest upon the battered duffel bag on the seat beside him.

Harmony's suggestion that the child was crying for that old doll didn't make sense.

He wasn't giving up that doll. It was all he had of Grace.

Shrimp was really glad they were coming home after two weeks of living in the Nevilles' bunkhouse, though it was a step above the Joels' tiny hired-hand cabin where they had spent the first two weeks of February. Staying at other ranchers while Jonah helped repair equipment, mend fence lines, and seed spring wheat, had social advantages, but generally Shrimp wanted her own sleeping rug in her own home. Home was home, where her dreams of Shep would be uninterrupted.

"Is this a meaningful conversation?" Jonah asked wryly as he lifted his fingers from the steering wheel to greet Jones's truck as it passed him. He wasn't mind-chatting with his dog;

he just knew Shrimp well enough to know she liked Shep and home.

The Emersons' teenage daughter had a dirty mind, hankering after him when he was stripped of his shirt. Of course, Jonah had read that in her expression, not her mind. Emily's sexual experiences exceeded her years.

Frank Neville worried about money, his wife would have to have an operation soon. Jonah had caught the desperation in his neighbor's—mind? He shook his head. Desperation was a facial expression...he'd understood Frank's expression or the tone of his voice, and had lowered his working price. The next second Jonah was asking Frank if he'd mind repaying him in ranch work hours, when it was convenient. Or if Frank chose, he could make the payments in stallion stud services, garden produce or any convenient payment. There was no hurry for Frank to repay him, but Jonah knew that the rancher's pride demanded payment.

After hearing his back teeth grind, Jonah forced his jaw to relax. There was no way facial expressions could explain other things. Like Mrs. Bonds exercising her feminine muscles while she was pushing her grocery cart. Like Doris Freeman, a seventy-year-old church matron, wanting to stir her husband into a froth or rather froth him with whipping cream.

Or Lucky meeting him in front of the old Grand Union Hotel and chatting about branding while he was thinking about playing bedroom lasso games with Harmony. "Games," Jonah muttered darkly.

When other people were near Jonah, he could sense... He shrugged lightly. He probably sensed people's thoughts. Living alone, it was reasonable that he understood basic human nature. After all, for ages Western men had spent hours contemplating the human mind over the campfire. Bartenders and cowboys were expert psychologists, and if he were to ask any of the old-timers about his problems, they'd all tell him the same thing—he was just plain "range squirrelly." They'd say he'd bottled his natural woman needs and they had backed up on him, thus causing an eventual terminal condition, "squirrelly." He'd get older and moldier and crazier and filled with strange malarkey and "bunk."

*He didn't understand or believe in mind-reading powers. If
he did believe, he wouldn't want them. He was just plain losing his mind and Harmony had somehow loosened another of
his mental screws.*

"Mental powers. Malarkey," Jonah muttered as he slowed
to turn under the Fargo ranch sign. As long as Harmony stayed
on her side of the fence and didn't bother him, he could manage. He'd always managed.

Jonah scanned his fields, the wheat fields he'd decided not
to work and the range grasslands. The cattle looked good; he'd
been checking on them with the help of a neighbor. His five
mares were grazing in the back field, the colt frisking around
the mare. The old house—

Jonah pushed down the clutch and the brake and quickly
reversed the pickup. He backed until he could see the Fargo sign
overhead.

Gleaming in the noonday sun, two wrought-iron cupids
fluttered above the Fargo name. With drawn bows, they
pointed arrows at each other. They were welded to the old sign
in a fancy scroll design.

Jonah glanced at the metal glinting from his rooftop and
then to the bright copper weather vane gleaming on top of his
barn. He looked back at the house, inhaled and slowly placed
his pickup in gear. "Shut up, Shrimp. It is not beautiful."

He stopped the pickup and leapt out onto the soggy ground.
He placed his hands on his hips and stared up at the cupid
weather vane, the little arrow pointing in the direction of the
late-March breeze. Jonah tipped back his hat and angled his
head. He moved three feet to one side, looking up at the lightning rods on top of his house. The dandy spiraling cupid design set off his new sheet-metal roof.

He jerked off his hat, whacked it against his thigh and looked
back to the Fargo sign. "The hell it perks the place up,
Shrimp," he stated darkly.

There he stood, his boots locked to Fargo land that had been
in his family since homesteading days. His forefathers had en-
dured Blackfoot attacks, outlaws and natural disasters. Now he
was surrounded by cupids on all three sides, and if given the
choice, he would have preferred an honest Blackfoot attack. He
jammed his hat down and whistled for his favorite mare. The

quickest way to face a cupid bushwhacker was to ride straight for her place and have it out. The old horse trail was faster than the road.

Priscilla, his mare, nickered a soft welcome just as a shiny new van pulled under the Fargo cupids. The van's side panels were emblazoned with the large logo Fascinating Homes.

Lucky's fancy black pickup pulled in behind the van; Jonah could see the cowboy's grin behind the windshield. A glossy city blonde stepped out of the van. She wanted pictures and an interview because of his unusual ranch and home ornaments; her readers would love the idea of cupids on a Montana ranch. "I've been calling on a regular basis, but you don't have a message machine. We'd so love to see the interior of your home...with the unusual decor outside, you probably have wonderful ideas to share in...that," she finished with a puzzled frown at Jonah's small weathered house with peeled paint.

Lucky was smirking. "Huh. Never knew you were a love god. Yep. That's what you are, Fargo. A pure piece of two-hundred-or-so pounds, six-foot-three, rough, tough, rodeo-bucking, one-hundred-percent love god."

Lilly Mason's four-wheeler eased under the cupids and stopped behind Lucky's pickup. Lilly leaned out of her window and asked, "Jonah, where did you get those beautiful cupids? I want Roy to put one up on the barn, just like yours. I know my married daughters will want the copper weather vane style on their houses, too."

The citizen's band in her rig crackled and Lilly picked up the speaker. "Better get over here, Susie. Jonah's place. He's going to be featured in a home decor magazine for the cupids he's got all over.... That's right...Jonah Fargo. He's got a cupid weather vane and cupids over the driveway sign...really good idea. You'd better get over here. If we hurry, we can be the first to get in on the cupids-house thing. We might set up a tour, a house to house cupid party. I'm going to be busy looking around, but get on the CB and get the girls over here."

"Mr. Fargo, do you think you could stand a little to the left for the photographer? He'd like to line up the cupid on the barn with your face.... Ah...do you think you could...ah...maybe smile a bit?" the city blonde asked too brightly.

"Sure, Jonah. Give her a real love-god smile," Lucky sing-songed with a big smirk.

Harmony lay soaking in her second chamomile bath of the day. Jonah's last cupid was in place at sunset the previous day and she had awakened with stiff, pained muscles. Pax's experience and his family and Lucky helped enormously. The cowboy seemed so eager to help, and even invited his friends over for the surprise she was preparing for Jonah. They built the scaffolding quickly, and seemed to relish the chore, eager for Jonah's return. The experienced men made easy work of the sheet-metal roofing. Lucky had grinned from the time he delivered the sheet-metal roofing at daybreak until the men's pickups departed under the new cupids on the Fargo sign.

Bathwater drizzled on her chest as she squeezed the bath sponge. Her debt to Jonah was finally paid and she could go on with her life.

She had missed Jonah, the black-hearted, gloomy, tough, lanky, evil-tempered yahoo. Harmony adjusted the folded towel beneath the nape of her neck and leaned her head back against the tile to examine her emotions concerning Jonah Fargo, cowboy cum psychic.

Shrouded in hard times and aching for his daughter, Jonah's powers had been stirred by his desperation. While she wished him well, realizing the agony of his discovery that he had powers, Harmony had very little patience with Jonah's attitudes, his ability to stir her emotions, or his take-care-of-this now tendencies.

Harmony did not want to think about making love with Jonah. She had lost enough sleep already, thinking about that man.

She patted the wild topknot of curls on her head and gave herself over to the soothing bath.

She'd created her best work and now her debt to Jonah was repaid.

Jonah? Coming here? He's angry? Harmony listened very carefully, the hairs on the nape of her neck rising. She heard his boots crossing the boards of her kitchen, her living room, muffled at times by the braided rugs. The purposeful thuds didn't sound as if he might be coming to thank her.

Harmony sank lower into the bathwater just as the door crashed open and Jonah stood glaring down at her. "Don't think you can hide in here, little sweetheart," he said in a deep, tight tone and moved into the room.

He plopped the toilet lid down and sat on it. He ripped off his leather gloves with the air of a man prepared to lay down laws.

"Would you mind waiting in the other room while I dry and dress?" Harmony asked tightly.

He scowled down at her, then whipped off his hat and plunked his gloves in it. He placed it over the bath powders and scents on a shelf. The feminine collection of bottles rattled ominously. "Yes, I would mind."

"Is there a problem?" she asked lightly.

"You got it." He watched Harmony draw the huge sponge over her chest and sink lower in the water. "All I want to know is who helped you."

Jonah had "vigilante" written all over his rugged, unshaven cheeks.

She liked his mustache. It was full and thick, definitely not squiggly. She'd never been kissed by a man with a mustache before, she thought suddenly.

"Who helped you?" he repeated. She was distantly glad that he was so angry; he hadn't read her thought about his new mustache. She'd never seen a mustache like that before, as if it belonged there, boldly matching Jonah's strong face.

"Do you like my work?" she asked slowly. He'd better, because she ached in every muscle, and the cupids were her best efforts in her career. She'd worked extra hours, fashioning them between preparing wind chimes and other smaller weather vanes for shipping to her customers. And she had deserted Therapy.

"Cupids," he snapped. "Cupids all over the place."

"Yes?" she inquired carefully.

"You can have them back, just as soon as I locate your accomplice and make him take them down. Now, who is he? Pax? No, Janice wouldn't let him do ladder work with that newly healed leg."

"You can't just barge in here and demand the names of my 'accomplices,' Jonah."

"Why can't I? Lucky just called me a 'love god,' and some city woman and photographer are invading my ranch. I must have had five local women stop and ask where I got my cupids." He gripped the sponge she had been holding, won the small tug-of-war easily, then tossed it into the bathroom sink. "Well?"

"Buckaroo, you are truly pushing me," Harmony said, crossing her arms and straining to keep her temper leashed.

"Good." His gaze drifted downward, brushing the cloudy water and bubbles lapping against her concealing hands. Then he slowly looked down the length of the tub until he found her toes.

She eased them down into the water, which only caused her knees to rise above the concealing milky water, and Jonah's gaze slid back to them. Harmony lowered her knees, settling for her toes' exposure to Jonah's very close scrutiny. His study of her returned slowly up the bathwater to look at her freshly washed hair pulled on top of her head.

Then his blue eyes shot a laserlike stare at her mouth, then her eyes. "We've got something running between us," he stated in a low, steady tone that caused her to shiver. "I don't like it."

"Cupids on your rooftops?" she prodded innocently, desperately wanting to avoid the electricity flowing between them. "You wanted the names of my helpers?" Her voice rose too high on her last words because Jonah was calmly rolling up his sleeves. "What are you doing?"

She saw a quick image of her nude, dripping body flopped over Jonah's shoulder.

"This." Then he bent and plucked her from the water, carried her into the bedroom and dumped her on the bed.

Harmony quickly reached for the hems of the quilt and flipped them over her body. She glared up at him. "We have nothing in common, other than your emerging powers... which you have, Jonah. There is nothing 'running' between us."

"I can't think of anything worse than a man-woman thing with you," he stated flatly.

"Likewise. You may leave now," she said regally, in her best dismissing tone. Jonah didn't leave time for her to study him, to sort out and prepare for his next move. When he was in her vicinity and acting like this, she had her hands—her mind—full of protecting herself. Whatever happened to the Harmony Davis who methodically planned her life?

"You've got circles under your eyes and you've lost weight."

She resented his notation of the obvious. "I work hard. It's my busy season. You're not looking so great yourself."

"I'll bring back your cupids. You can sell them and save yourself some work."

"You will not. They are my masterpieces . . . my final payments on my debt. You saved my life, remember?" *There was no way she could have bonded with Jonah Fargo.* She was far too sensible and cautious, and the irate, tough cowboy in front of her didn't suit any of her requirements for a relationship— if she were looking.

There is no way I could have made love to her, Jonah thought grimly. *I'd sooner get thrown in a pit of snakes.*

Been seeing June lately? she tossed back, and belatedly recognized that he was calmer now, receiving thoughts.

Jonah inhaled sharply, then very firmly began prying away the shielding quilt. When Harmony batted at him, he held her wrists in one hand and pinned her squirming body on the bed with the flat of his other hand on her stomach. "Let me go, Jonah," she ordered, her heart racing as he looked down her body, his eyes darkening.

"This is what's real, not fairies and crystal balls," he said bitterly. "I don't want any ties with you past this. And right now, it's a powerful need, rosebud."

Rosebud. The name shocked Jonah, his hands trembled. Then his fingers locked over her femininity, pressing gently, and his eyes closed. *Rosebud.*

He frowned deeply, as though trying to remember. His uncertainty and agony swirled around her and she ached to hold him close to her. The bells on her wrist tinkled as Jonah's thumb caressed her wrist.

Harmony tried to balance the emotions storming in the quiet bedroom. He was seeing her again, holding her again, making her a part of him and testing the images against reality as she lay beneath his hands.

Jonah slowly sat on the bed and, with his eyes closed, eased his hands to fit over her breasts. He touched her gently, seeking the hardened tips with his thumbs, then he inhaled sharply and stood. "If you want me, you don't have to splash cupids on my property. Just give me a call."

Harmony lay still on the bed, winded by Jonah's touch, his quick emotions . . . her unsteady needs as she realized that Jonah had reclaimed his hat and was standing at her bedroom door watching her.

She couldn't let him get away with that arrogant, pleased expression as if he'd had the last word.

Harmony gripped the bells on her wrist and prayed that she could keep the temper that only Jonah could arouse.

"I suppose that fire-hot woman look of yours means you'll be welding on Therapy again," he drawled. "Clumping around in your workboots and wishing you could have me."

"Ohh . . ." Harmony, who liked a harmonious life and comfortable people, launched herself at him.

He thrust out his hand, staying her. Because she was new in the physical attack business, she wondered about her first strike zone. Jonah looked as tough as granite. While she was wondering, he stripped away his shirt and stuffed her into it.

Come on, rosebud, she heard his thoughts taunt her.

With the tiny bit of control she still possessed, Harmony slammed her bedroom door shut. It helped to muffle the sound of Jonah's chuckle.

She stared at the door, listening to the deep masculine sound that became roaring laughter.

Seven

―――

"Buckaroo, I'll come after my cupids. If you don't appreciate great art, someone else will. I don't want you to keep anything that you don't want. I'll find another way to repay you. I'll be coming after them," Harmony repeated in a low, trembling, husky tone as she jerked open her bedroom door.

She dismissed the sound of her bracelet's tiny alarm system. When Jonah was around her, her calm aura seemed to require higher maintenance than she possessed. Tiny bells on her wrist weren't enough.

"No, you won't come near their bare backsides. I've decided to hold them hostage," Jonah said, controlling his need to grin. He felt strong, light, and back to plain old good. Harmony, in a lather, did put a pretty shine on his love-god problems. She looked delicious in his shirt, which reached her knees. Jonah studied her legs; she had really pretty knees. He thought about her sitting on his lap at Christmas. "Don't worry. When Christmas comes, I'll put twinkle lights on them."

"Why? Why are you holding them hostage?" Harmony stalked into the living room, jamming his shirtsleeves up higher on her arms. The heavy froth of her damp hair tumbled down to her shoulders and she blew away a spiraling curl that had lodged on her nose.

Jonah drew on his leather gloves. "You bring that crew of desecraters to my place and we'll talk."

He frowned, belatedly remembering a quick impression when Lucky had arrived at the Fargo ranch. Lucky had been proud of his handiwork.

"Talk?"

"Not any of the mental communications stuff you spout. We'll decide the rules of living in the same area…after I teach them a lesson or two about invading and welding graffiti to a man's property."

"You are not using violence on the people who helped me. You'll have to go through me first. And my cupids are not graffiti," she shot back, bending to pick up a crystal ball as though she were going to throw it at him.

"You'll have to come after them. Think of them as unloved little orphans." Jonah liked the idea of Harmony coming to him.

Harmony's eyebrows shot up. "They require care. I'll send you instructions—or I'll come tend them myself."

"No visitation rights until this is settled. There won't be any bare backside polishing on my rooftops until I say so." Jonah studied his leather gloves and flexed his fingers. He was getting to her and savoring it. He hadn't played or teased for an eternity. Getting under Harmony's skin was little payback for the sleepless nights he'd had dreaming of her in that skimpy nightie and Santa Claus cap. At least now she wasn't saying in that imperial tone, "You may leave now."

"*You may leave now*" was pretty hard on a man who felt like a bridegroom the morning after his wedding night. Even if their lovemaking was a dream, she ought to have treated him more gently.

Jonah tightened his lips and the cords of his jaw ached with tension. He was not a sensitive man, but there were limits.

"I did not bruise you," Harmony stated shakily. "I have never hurt anyone in my life."

He flexed his fingers again, enjoying the passion rising in her; she went to his head. He discarded that thought—he had enough problems in his head. Harmony just made him feel good. He could feel her revving up, the emotions swirling around her, fire lighting her golden eyes and shimmering in the reddish lights of her hair. "Yep. Unloved little orphans, that's what they'll be. Standing out there in their birthday suits, icicles hanging from their little bows and arrows and birds—"

"Jonah!" she exclaimed in a tone of pure indignation and hurled the crystal ball at him.

He caught it neatly, hefted it thoughtfully, then placed it on her countertop. The crystal ball represented her psychic theories. He had enjoyed his skirmish with her, really enjoyed it. But he didn't trust himself to look at her again. He was getting that loving feeling, like a man who needed a second helping of a really good first event. The crystal ball reminded him of reality—Harmony wasn't for him. "Ma'am," he said solemnly, nodding and placed his hand on her doorknob, preparing to leave.

"Jonah, you can't leave like that," Harmony stated unevenly behind him.

"Why not?" His body tensed, his senses alerted. A really nice dream about this time would be for Harmony to wrap her arms around him and invite him into her boudoir, like a good dream-bride should. But that wasn't going to happen, and what was he doing feeling bruised and discarded anyway? Making love to Harmony had only been a dream and not a very smart one at that.

After almost three months of her "You may leave now," he was still reeling from that cursed dream.

"Uh...it's fairly warm outside, almost April, but uh...Jonah, you aren't wearing a shirt. You could catch cold."

His fingers tightened on the doorknob, his body tensing. He turned slowly to her. Though she was angry with him, Harmony was a softhearted lady. "That's because *you're* wearing it," he said very reasonably.

She shifted restlessly within the loose folds of the shirt and glanced down at it in surprise. "Oh! Yes, I am. Wait a minute. I'll change," she said airily, inching toward her bedroom door.

"No other woman has ever worn my shirts," Jonah stated, responding to the impulse that had just hit him. Now where would he get an idea she didn't want to wear another woman's leftovers?

"You certainly stuffed me into it like you knew what you were doing," she said, eyeing him warily as he took two steps toward her.

"I'm a fast mover." When her eyes locked to his chest, the taut muscles on his arms, Jonah realized that he was flexing his muscles. He instinctively knew that Harmony was fascinated by the line of his body. She wanted to place her hand on him, trace the flow of his muscles and— He watched the delicate swallow move down her throat and the tiny bells on her wrist jingled merrily.

Oh, no... He heard a low, husky feminine voice mourn. Yet Harmony's lips hadn't moved, the bottom one was trembling too much.

"You sure look ripe," Jonah heard himself murmuring in a deep, husky voice. "As sweet as dew sparkling like little jewels in the dawn. That or a rosebud bouquet about to open to full glory. I'd say you could be a real steamy, hothouse rose if—"

"Uh ... let's stay on track here," she said breathlessly, after a full two seconds and several disbelieving blinks. She took another step back from him. When her back hit the wall, she gasped slightly. "Let's be reasonable and do some clear thinking."

He sensed her desperation and fought the laughter tugging at his lips. She made him feel good; it had been forever since a woman was desperate around him, and he'd never known a woman as nervous as Harmony was with him right now. That was good because the feeling was mutual, and he didn't want her to be disadvantaged when they came to a showdown. The sunlight shimmered in her hair as she said, "Let's get back to the part about how I am going to retrieve my lost orphans ... er ... ah ... my cupids."

"Did anyone ever tell you that you think too much?" he asked, lifting a damp curl with his leather-covered finger and studying it.

"Thinking is good," she stated evenly. "Thinking is very good to sort out problems, analyze them and—" Then she closed her eyes, inhaled and flushed as he thought about how he'd like to love her from the top of her head to the bottom of her feet.

"You're flustered and very warm," Jonah noted and realized suddenly that when Harmony's emotions were ruling her, he wasn't that sensitive to her thoughts. Of course, he corrected warily, her expressions were clear-cut definers of her moods. Because she was so horrified that she had thrown the crystal ball, so uncertain of her need to touch him right now, to hold him, Jonah carefully folded her in his arms.

Without her clear-thinking cloak and her quiet, peaceful aura, Harmony required delicate care. Jonah eased off his gloves while she was trembling, rigid in his arms. She needed petting, and cuddling, and holding and reassurance and sweet talk. He could almost hear her think. She'd been more emotional than she'd ever been; she was shaken in the aftermath and fearing being near him. Being near him was disaster. She could handle the situation.... No, she couldn't. Her legs were too weak and in another minute—

He understood her emotions. It wasn't every day that a man like him folded the other part of himself into his heart. Like a sweet, yet aching homecoming. He stroked her back gently and rocked her against him and treasured her heartbeat racing against his. Whoever Mark was, he should have treated Harmony better.

"I don't want this," she whispered against his shoulder.

"Okay," he agreed slowly, continuing to rock and to smooth her back. If Harmony were really his and they were approaching their second lovemaking, he didn't know if he could restrain himself this time. Harmony trembled in his arms and Jonah nuzzled the fast-beating little vein in her temple; she was in a panic, her emotions in turmoil. She began focusing on the fit of their bodies, the dual pressure of her breasts exotic against him.

Her hands opened to slide around his back and Jonah knew his heart had stopped beating as her fingertips settled lightly on his skin. "You'll catch cold if you go outside without your shirt," she worried aloud, her fingers fluttering across his shoulders. Her hands locked to his upper arms.

"I'm a tough old buzzard," he whispered gently as her hands explored the muscles of his back. He shifted slightly, drawing her softness against his chest and closing his eyes, relishing the fit of her against him.

"Mmm. How tough?" she asked, her lips warm against his skin.

"Well, maybe I'm more sweet and lovable than tough," he teased, and her lips curved against his throat.

"You're hopeless."

"I know. Hopeless through and through, that's what I am," Jonah agreed easily. He slid his hands under her shirt and eased them to settle on her backside. Just one word, one look from her and he'd leave. . . .

Harmony stood very still as Jonah breathed lightly, fearing she'd step away. If this was a dream, he was riding it to the end. She wiggled closer, her arms tightening around him. "You're not going anywhere. You started this and you can finish it."

"You are a strong woman, Harmony Davis," he murmured appreciatively, filling his palms with her backside and caressing her. "I suppose if I ran, you might bulldog me like that metal monster."

"I could desecrate you," she threatened with a ripple of laughter as she remembered his discomfort. She hadn't known that a man could look so hungry and desperate when he was watching the flow of her hand that day.

Of course he noticed her hand stroking her monster; the movement had fascinated him and made his body harden. He kissed her palm and Harmony inhaled sharply. Whoever this Mark character was, he wasn't into the finer points of treating a lady tenderly.

He didn't want to think about whoever Mark was or what he had done with Harmony; Jonah didn't want Harmony thinking about anyone but him right now. He knew that she was scrambling now for what she held dear, logic and nonlogic. He knew she wanted to tuck her emotions into a neat pocket and button it closed.

"You're all threats and no action. I'll be wearing a long beard and cobwebs before you pick through whatever is holding you back. Desecrate away," he invited, kissing her cheek and finding her mouth.

Harmony reached for him and met his mouth with hers.

She wanted him desperately to complete her soul, her heart, her body. Jonah was the missing part of her, and nothing could keep her from him now. She felt fierce and strong and wild, claiming what was hers, what was destined to be hers. . . .

"I want to look at you, rosebud," he whispered unevenly, his hand trembling, sliding to rest between her breasts.

Harmony trapped his hand and shivered, her lips poised beneath his. She was desperate for him, for his strength to fill her, to complete the emptiness. "Why?"

"It's a love-god thing," Jonah murmured in a teasing tone against her lips, biting them gently. "We love gods like to see our desserts before we nibble on them."

"Oh...I had other plans." She looked at him sharply. "Are you teasing me, Jonah?"

"Sure am. Feels good, too. You can't have everything your way, driving this rig too fast and not smelling the grass." Jonah shuddered, his hand moving over her breast.

"That's roses, Jonah," she corrected with a grin. "Smell the roses."

"Uh-huh. Come here, rosebud." Then he picked her up and carried her to the bed as if nothing could keep them apart.

That was exactly what Harmony wanted; he sensed her need for him in the small shadowy room. But as Jonah lowered her onto the bed, she had to ask, "Are you afraid to make love with me?"

"Mark isn't in this bed," Jonah said unevenly. "Now, do something fierce and loving, just like you look, rosebud."

So she grabbed his shoulders and bulldogged him beneath her. In the next frantic seconds, she hugged him while he tugged off his boots. She pressed her breasts to him and held him while he struggled with his jeans. Then Jonah's mouth was at her breasts, the buttons of the shirt tearing free as they strained to get closer.

Then he was hers, this magnificent . . . love god, taking care to sheath himself in protection. Harmony wiggled closer to him, caught him with her arms and legs and tender muscles and held him tightly. Jonah's hands gripped her bottom firmly and he arched against her, joining them deeply.

He paused, luxuriating in the soft warmth, in the tight clasp of her body around his.

Then Harmony began to giggle and Jonah frowned. "This isn't supposed to be a laughing moment, rosebud," he said unsteadily, his frown fierce.

But she was too happy, too filled with delight and wonder and Jonah. She eased slowly down to lay upon him and snuggled her face into his warm throat. She moved her hips against his, relished the fit of him inside her. He groaned deeply as she smoothed his cheek with hers. She nuzzled his throat, his temples and kissed his nose. "Can't a girl be happy when she captures a love god?"

Jonah began to smile slowly, enchanting her. Then his kisses were so soft, so tender, his hands stroking her gently, cherishing her.

The first storm hit her without warning, tightening her body and flinging her at him. While she reeled with the deep heat, the power that was Jonah, his mouth suckling at her breast, another ripple hit her. The ultimate sensations were so strong and perfect that she stilled, cherishing the delight bursting within her, prolonging the pleasure. The next heartbeat, she was hungry, unable to control the desperate need to be closer to Jonah, to hold him and make him a part of her, capturing, releasing, only to capture again.

There was light and pulsing and pleasure bursting within her, and Jonah was there, secure, urging her on, staying with her, her mate, her bonded lover, the very essence of her soul....

He breathed heavily, turning her beneath him and kissing her lips. She saw herself filling his darkened eyes, the desire and the hunger riding high between them.

Had he given himself to her so fully, so beautifully? Had she taken and given her essence, her heat back to him?

Had they bonded, shattered and dissolved? Even now Jonah was refilling her, hungry again.

She caught his tongue, suckled it and moved her body along his, taking, giving ... closer....

She cried out at the pinnacle of their love, her eyes widening as Jonah braced, giving himself to her. She strained higher, catching him, holding him tight, and knew this was how a man should love a woman, the fierce heat and intensity riveting them, forging them together beyond this moment.

Then when Jonah eased, his eyes tender upon her, she gathered him to her and cradled him.

How sweet this was, Jonah's heavy weight lying upon her, his face resting in the cove of her shoulder and throat and his body still a part of hers. He kissed her gently, soothingly, his hands smoothing, cherishing, while his heart slowed against hers. They had run fiercely to the deep mating of souls and bodies, and now there would be rest.

She sighed, content now against him, her need temporarily satisfied because she knew that she would need him again, and he would gather her even more tenderly against him as though claiming her forever.

Jonah stroked her breasts, kissed them, savored them slowly and she floated gently in the scent of him, the warm strength so close and tender.

"I don't know what to do now," he murmured sleepily, easing away slightly, and stroking her hair back from her damp cheek. "Because I sure don't want to wake up alone."

She was too exhausted to think, so she settled close to him, resting her head on his shoulder. Jonah's hand cupped her breast, his legs tangled intimately with hers.

Was she awake or was she dreaming? she wondered as Jonah gathered her back against him, his thighs hard beneath hers. "Shh," he whispered, comforting her with the newness of sharing her bed and what had passed between them. He caressed her breasts lazily and she realized that night had settled into her house, gently, softly, even as Jonah was making her a part of him again.

This time the loving was dreamy, warm, soothing and yet wild and fierce. She realized sleepily that she caught him close, her nails digging slightly into his back, her teeth biting his shoulder. She gave herself to the ultimate, untethered delight of making love with him.

The shower's hot water sluiced down Jonah's sated body. He raised his face to the pulsing water and tried to think.

When a man awoke in a woman, the loving already beginning naturally, it wasn't a dream.

Harmony lay sleeping in her bed, tousled from making love with him. The marks and the tiny bites on his shoulder weren't caused by a dream. When she'd arched against him in a tense, loving, heated frenzy, he'd burst, the tight knot of loneliness coming unfurled. This time she loved him with more certainty, taking, demanding. This time... The time before was a dream. Or was it?

He wasn't leaving before she awoke and until he had some answers. He dried quickly and entered the bedroom. Since apparently they'd shared real lovemaking, he could sleep until she awoke.

In her sleep, Harmony moved into his arms as naturally as if she'd been his wife for years. She rested a moment, then sighed reluctantly and eased away, leaving the bed to shower.

She reentered the bedroom and slid into bed, snuggling close to him and sighing as though she'd never moved away.

Jonah prayed the child wouldn't start crying before he dealt with Harmony.

"Harmony..." Jonah was saying as she tried to snuggle deeper into her sleep. She lay on her stomach because the muscles on her backside ached. "Harmony, wake up."

"No." She didn't want to leave what had happened; she wanted to wallow and revel in the wonder and the beauty of Jonah's loving. She groaned slightly as she moved, her roof-climbing muscles protesting and her intimate muscles slightly aching. She wanted to stay wrapped in Jonah's warmth, his scent, and reached to gather her pillow closer to her. She snuggled in her nest, fitting the night's memories around her and easing the pillow gently under her tender breasts.

She inhaled, the muscles of her arms, back and legs tight and protesting the movement. Lifting and welding her cupids to Jonah's rooftops had pushed her strength to the limit. She opened her eyes, looked at the four posts of her bed and flushed as she remembered how she had...had...thrown herself into lovemaking. She'd taken Jonah, claimed him in the most primitive way for her mate.

They were bonded now. Or at least she had bonded with him.

She breathed quietly as Jonah's weight shifted the mattress beneath her.

He was thinking; she could feel his questions thrusting at her; the room hummed with Jonah's thoughts. They slid by her too quickly; she couldn't grasp the shifting directions. Was he sorry? Was he afraid of her now? Had she taken too much?

Her fingers gripped the pillow as Jonah leaned down to lay his cheek along hers. "You must have strained something, planting those cupids on my ranch," he whispered huskily in a deep, sensual tone that caught her broadside and pushed her alert buttons. "You've been groaning a bit."

She'd purred a bit, too, last night as he held her. And she had the prettiest little surprised scream when she... Jonah was thinking.

"I do not scream," Harmony stated unsteadily. Couldn't he at least show her the courtesy of lining up her ducks or summoning her defenses against him? "Ah...Jonah, if you would step into the living room, I'll be out in a minute."

He nuzzled her shoulder, his beard rough and delicious against her skin. "No, rosebud. We're going to talk right here, where we made love and where I'd like to make love again...."

She must not have frightened him too badly if he wanted a repeat performance. She tried to grab the sheet he was slowly drawing off her backside. "Ah...Jonah, I really need to get dressed—"

She inhaled sharply as Jonah's gentle, callused hands moved over her shoulders, massaging them, his fingers finding the hurting knots and working them gently. He smoothed her back, massaging her while she tried not to give in to the wonderful luxury.

Humor laced his deep drawl. "It's good to know that you won't be clumping around your monster this morning."

"I just may," she returned challengingly.

"Uh-huh. Your little groans say something else."

When Jonah found the taut muscles across her shoulders, she muffled the next luxurious little groan in her pillow.

Jonah patted her bottom affectionately, then worked his way down to the backs of her thighs. Harmony shivered and squirmed. Their intimacy was too new.

Jonah leaned down, nibbled on her ear and kissed her hot cheek. She sensed an alert humming in him as he said, "Don't start that thinking business now, rosebud. Just tell me, who is Mark? Because he's not coming into our bed again."

"Our bed?" Did he know she would never join, never bond with anyone after him? "Ah . . . Jonah . . . yes, we need to talk this through, but ah . . . I'd like to dress. Since you're already dressed, I feel a bit disadvantaged."

"I like it this way right now," he returned firmly. Jonah continued to rub her legs, concentrating on the tight muscles of her calves. He was thinking, delving into and recalling their conversations.

"You haven't said anything about a Mark to me. Pax hasn't said the name, either. How did I know that Mark was a part of your life?" he asked slowly, his hand opening and caressing her bottom.

"Mark is my ex-husband." Jonah held her still gently, firmly when she tried to squirm away.

Jonah was too quiet; Harmony could feel him tense, felt his withdrawal from her. Her heart tore slowly, painfully, as he gently covered her with the sheet as though he were placing what had happened in the past, behind a locked door. The crying child hovered around him and Harmony knew that he had awakened to the mournful sound.

"I felt like we'd made love before this time," Jonah said slowly, smoothing her hair.

"Yes."

"What do you mean, 'yes'? Exactly how could we have made love before yesterday without me knowing it?" The desperation rimming his voice caused her to ache. She gathered the pillow to her, shielding her aching breasts and eased to sit as she took his hand.

Not to be denied, Jonah slid his hand beneath the pillow, cupping her breast, testing its shape and weight. Then his touch slid down, flattened over her stomach, his fingers curling firmly over her. "You were afraid last time and you're still shy of me," he murmured unevenly.

"You held back last time, but you didn't this time," she whispered as he studied her, looking beyond the textures, the warmth and his humming, yet suppressed desire for her.

He was sorting through his thoughts, his memories, shuffling them like cards, trying to find order and reasons. "That night I fell asleep here?"

"Yes." Harmony placed her hand along his cheek, cradling the rugged contours as she ached to hold him, to shelter him from pain.

His face lined with pain, his throat trying to swallow. "No. I woke up in my clothes. I've never loved like that, Harmony. Like I was claiming my other half, my bride. I dreamed I was in a flame with you."

She eased a dark shaft of hair from his lined brow. "Yes. Just like that. A claiming."

Jonah, be careful. Don't try to understand ... just accept. ...

I'm losing my mind, he thought desperately, his fingers finding the delicate marks on his shoulders—her claiming of him.

You knew about Mark because you read my thoughts.

Why was her ex-husband afraid of her? Jonah studied her, his expression dark and tight.

He knew I had powers. I frightened him. ...

Powers? She had powers ... no, she said I have powers ... that extrasensory baloney.

"If you can read my mind," Jonah asked slowly, feeling as though he were stepping through a loaded mine field.

"Mind field," Harmony corrected gently and tried a little smile to warm his grim awakening.

"A little like an invasion of privacy, isn't it? I mean even if it was true?"

"I wasn't too happy stepping into your planned interlude with June when you picked me up that day."

Jonah's eyebrows shot up, then lowered into a fierce frown. "What?"

"I believe a nice way of putting it would be that you were on your way to drown your problems in June's bed. She was your last resort. You'd reached the end of your endurance, you needed sleep badly and you were ready to try drastic measures," Harmony said as gently as she could. It wasn't easy admitting to seeing his thoughts about another woman.

"If you were in my mind just then—not that it's possible— but say it was ... it would be like a ménage à trois, isn't that right?" he asked darkly.

She blushed and shivered. "I wasn't a participant. You were doing the plotting."

Jonah considered this, traveling over that day in his mind. A dark red flush moved up his cheeks and the muscle in his jaw tensed repeatedly. She was fascinated by him, this blushing man, her mate, her other half. Her sweet Mr. Ho Ho.

Her tenderness tilted, lashed by Jonah's dark stormy mood, bristling, ill-tempered buckaroo-macho thoughts about men not blushing. Women were sweet and shy and *they* blushed— but not full-grown men. He hadn't heard the name Mr. Ho Ho. Yes, he had, that time at Christmas.... Jonah ran his trembling fingers through his hair. "You mean, you sat there in my pickup and tapped into—okay, tried to tap into—"

He was getting angry again, confused, hurting, aching with realities and nonrealities. But Harmony wasn't too pleased about admitting to jumping onto Jonah's sexual plans for June Fields.

"It had been so long, little sweetheart, that I had to plan out my moves," Jonah stated aloud, in his defense. "A man forgets things."

You certainly didn't forget anything yesterday. You were quite thorough, and if you had a plan I didn't know it.... You just reached...

Because you think too much, that's why. By the time you get through lining up your aura or ducks or whatever, taking everything nice and calm... Then Jonah scowled at her and smiled tightly. "But that control business doesn't work with me, does it? You like to be in control, keep things moving along smoothly, don't you? You don't like to have your feathers ruffled and you avoid showdowns. You're scared now, aren't you? Because you let go of the tiger-woman that no other man has seen. You wanted...you took, and nothing was according to schedule. Including those tiny red marks on my back and shoulders. Right now, you're slightly...."

Jonah leveled a mocking look at her. "Aghast. Yes, *we* are slightly unnerved, are we not?"

"That's enough," she managed as the anger clouds swirled around her. Jonah was too unsettling, too certain of himself, though his reading of her was on target. *I can't think when you...when you...start with me,* she admitted in her defense. *I like order and quiet, peace and tranquillity. Not that you'd have any idea about the definitions of those words, buckaroo.*

When a lady slaps her brand on a man, like posting her handiwork all over his ranch, she'd better watch it, Jonah thought threateningly.

"Holding cupids as hostages isn't civilized," Harmony stated righteously aloud.

"Do the words *bonding* and *mating* make sense to you? I mean, something about you and me?" he said tightly, as though daring her to say they did.

She sat very straight and allowed herself just one tiny shiver. "Do I look like a dictionary?" *If you don't know, I am certainly not explaining bonding and mating to you.*

"Do you know a Mr. Ho Ho?" he demanded, plowing right into another mental field before she finished with the current topic. "Someone likable...laughs a lot...overweight guy?"

"As in Santa Claus?" she singsonged and blinked innocently.

"I'm leaving," Jonah stated abruptly after closing his eyes. He wished he were in the past century, hiding out with nice, safe outlaws. One thing was certain, he wouldn't lasso and bulldog this little off-center sweetheart. Then his thoughts jumbled and became images, like erotic feminine fingers smoothing and grasping Therapy's horn.

"I am *not* off centered," Harmony muttered, nettled because she was the only one who thought their lovemaking was deeply meaningful.

Then after a long searching look, he was gone. She listened to the sound of his boots crossing her floors again, just as he had entered her home the day before.

"Fine, just fine. One love god escaping into the sunset absolutely free to roam the range, bonding and mating wherever. Take yourself away to your Motown bog. Forget about what happened between yesterday and now, and don't call me 'rosebud,'" Harmony muttered, drawing the edge of the sheet high to dry the tear trailing down her cheek. "Suits me, Mr. Ho Ho. And take care of my cupids."

Eight

The middle of April was fine fighting and revenge-on-Jonah weather. After two weeks of saturating too many handkerchiefs and pillowcases with her tears and cuddling Therapy, Harmony had pasted herself together with revenge glue. It was now two and a half weeks since Jonah had breached her emotional castle, took her heart captive, then swashbuckled out again. That half week had given her a new dimension and she'd pulled herself out of the weeping bog onto a road headed straight for revenge on Jonah.

One tiny, caring "How's it going, kid?" call from Jonah would have gone a long way in soothing her emotions. She'd laminated her soul, mind, body and heart for a lifetime to Jonah. After two weeks of heart shredding and waiting for Jonah to initiate a discussion during their uneasy truce, she had flipped on her ignition and had declared war.

Jonah had lessons to learn. Like the etiquette of loving and leaving, and sensitivity to others. She would teach him a necessary lesson—when a woman opened her heart to him, claimed him with her soul and her body, he shouldn't walk out and not check back for a damage report.

"I've never seen you on the revenge trail," Pax remarked with a joyful smirk. "It's pretty interesting. From what I see, you're devouring food and losing weight. You are very emotional now, Harmony. Hmm... Nice, cool Harmony on a rampage. You usually avoid explosive situations—"

"There is no way to avoid Jonah, Pax," Harmony stated darkly. "He's too big and too arrogant and too—"

"Sweet? Lovable? Romantic?" Pax provided, then winked at his sister. "Be careful. You could bruise him. He's been very sensitive when I mention your name. Looks at me like I'm going to accuse him of something and he isn't sure what. Funny thing...you take such care to plan your life...avoid using your powers or calling attention to yourself. I can't imagine why you want to 'teach Jonah a lesson.' After seeing you drown your problems or rather, stuff yourself during the Mark episode—"

"I was married to Mark, remember? Wives battle for a marriage, big brother. My problem with Jonah is entirely different. He requires head-on handling. He's too arrogant, and this whole countryside has been babying him, letting him do just as he likes," Harmony said, pausing to listen to her new CB crackling as Dora Wainwright discussed where she wanted to place her cupid.

"We let him do what he wants because he's sweet," Pax singsonged with a wide grin.

"Whatever. His time is up, though. He's messed with the wrong person." She was done weeping day and night, her body feeling listless without its missing part. Jonah had walked into her life, plucked her from her nice calming chamomile bath and had spent the night with her. The afternoon and the night and part of the morning, she corrected. A mini-honeymoon, sort of. Or was it a honeymoon for her and playtime for him? She had been loved and left because he couldn't handle reality. Or nonreality and his abilities. Well, Jonah had abilities—other than his lovemaking techniques—and it wasn't her fault. He could have called her and explained his doubts about their relationship. She could understand that a person's actions and thoughts could be drastically affected when they realized they had powers. "Everyone has let him do exactly as he wants, but I'm not going to," she repeated.

Pax's eyebrows lifted. "*Let* Jonah do what he wants? *Let?*" he said incredulously. "He just does what he thinks is best and usually helps those people around him."

"Ha! Then he's using emotional blackmail. Take a note, Pax. I have plans, big plans. I will not let Jonah off easily."

"My, my. I wonder why not? You're in a snit, little sister. Hmm…unusual for someone who sheds emotional distress and potential life mates—"

"Stop pointing that out. And do not use my name and Jonah's name in the same thought as you use life mate. *He…is…not…my…heart mate.*"

Harmony interrupted the ranchwives' rapid CB conversation about new rooftop decor at Fort Benton. "Breaker. This is the cupid maker. Why don't you go over to the Fargo place and check out the lightning-rod design?"

Pax sipped his herbal tea and grinned at her while she encouraged the ladies to rendezvous at Jonah's cupid exhibit—her best work. She wouldn't take orders or talk to customers who hadn't spent time at the Fargo ranch, observing the cupids, especially the weather vane acting in the wind. The ladies might consider adding personalized initials to the cupids.

"Revenge?" Pax asked, his golden eyes sparkling. "You've never been a revenge-seeking woman, Harmony. Or an especially angry one. Not even when Mark's true colors were revealed."

"Stop nudging me. Mark is not Jonah Fargo," she stated firmly, pouring more herbal tea from her grandmother's china teapot. She replaced the tea cozy as her grandmother had instructed her to do. She had always been sensible, doing what was expected of her. Until Jonah. She munched on her fifth raisin-and-nut cookie, Janice's specialty. "And Jonah Fargo's true colors are not sweet. I wanted to pay him back for saving my life and what did I get?"

She glanced at Pax, flushed, and carefully shielded her thoughts with plans of her next addition to Therapy's mane. The mane would be twisted metal cords adding light and movement that would match the tail. She watched Pax and knew he'd never sort through the twisted maze of metal mane, so she could think clearly until he unscrambled her camouflage.

Harmony regretted every aching moment in the two weeks that she had spent snuggled next to Therapy. The black metal monster had reminded her of Jonah, big and unshakable. This last half week, she'd slept in her bed and cuddled her pillow.

"So what's this about Therapy's horn? Or was that 'horny'?" Pax asked, picking up portions of her flying thoughts. His readings were getting faster since she had arrived.

"I refuse to sink to the level of your mentality." Harmony stood abruptly, bumping the table, as she took her cup and saucer to the sink. Her energy levels seemed unusually high, humming with the need to avenge her nights of crying over Jonah.

She was through with mourning the event, rather the several notable events. There would be no more bonding and mating thoughts involving Mr. Fargo. She focused on sweet revenge.

Jonah's dark ominous voice shot from the CB. "I heard that, little sweetheart, cupid maker. What's the idea of making my ranch into your advertisement catalog?" he demanded.

The cup and saucer rattled in her hands before she lowered them to the table. Harmony allowed herself a pleased, tight smirk. She'd been waiting for her bait to draw him from his hermit hole.

Her boots clumped on the way to the CB's microphone; she jerked it to her lips, jabbed the speaker button down and stated very distinctly, "*This is not 'little sweetheart.'* My buyers need to see the real product before they place their orders. You have possession, don't you, buckaroo?"

"I'm keeping it, too," he shot back. "You know what to do to get them back." Then his CB clicked off.

Harmony simmered for a full moment. "It's just like him to turn off his CB rather than discuss this like two adults. He's holding my poor cupids as his hostages. There's no telling what damage the birds are doing to them. My weather-vane design won't support an eagle's weight, you know."

"Discuss this problem like two *psychic* adults." Pax said, grinning.

Jonah's CB crackled on. "Come around suppertime if you can and bring something to eat to put me in a good mood. I like peach pie."

"Not today, dear. I have a headache," she said too sweetly, and blinked at Pax's roaring laughter.

"Are your desecraters having tea over there?" Jonah asked sharply after a static silence.

"It's a party, and you're not invited."

"Fine. I've got my cupids for company, don't I? Sprinkle sugar over that pie when you bake it, will you?" Then his machine clicked off again.

Harmony gripped her microphone tightly and tapped her work boot. The clumping rhythmic sound pacified her taut nerves and the tension humming in her body. "I hate that... when he gets the last word in."

"I bonded with Janice the minute I met her," Pax began slowly, his lips still touched by laughter. "She said it was love, but I knew nothing would separate us in this lifetime."

Harmony shot him a be-quiet stare. "*I did not bond with Jonah Fargo.* Did you remember to tell Amy Lodge to drop by Jonah's and take all her friends?"

"No need to. She saw your ad in the newspaper. Nice little map directing everyone to the Fargo place if they didn't know where it was."

"I thought it was a neat touch."

"Not too bad for someone who has just gotten into the revenge business. But I don't believe for a minute that there's not more to this story than Jonah keeping your cupids hostage."

"'Graffiti,' he called them," Harmony muttered. "My cupids are beautiful."

Jonah's radio crackled. In the background, Shrimp howled mournfully, aching for calmer times and better companions. "Pax? Tell your little sister that she's not getting away with this. You ought to see the females climbing all over this place.... My gosh, sweet heaven on Saturday, Aunt Sue's shoes, outside my window right now, there are the whole eight Peace-Jewel sisters—Opal, Diamond... the whole herd of them are standing around my barn. They filled three vans and brought their daughters and grandkids."

"Has June turned up yet?" Harmony asked too innocently.

"Anytime, little sweetheart," Jonah crooned in a come-and-get-it warning. "Anytime you're ready."

"He sounds tired," Pax said when Harmony plopped down, picked up her cup and began to study her tea leaves. "Has he resolved his daughter's death? Is he recognizing his powers?"

Harmony swirled her tea leaves out of the shape that designated love. "How should I know? I explained it to him. I can't make him open his locked-door mentality."

"Though he doesn't realize his potential, Jonah comes from a strong, old line of powers," Pax stated slowly. "He is your match . . . if he becomes aligned with himself."

"Don't worry about his alignment," Harmony said, resenting the sadness closing in around her heart. She'd been aligned very closely with Jonah Fargo and the encounter left her with a bleeding heart. She sniffed and brushed away a tear and looked out into the bright April sunlight. "Just keep him away from me."

"Love isn't that easy, little sister. You can't will it away, explain it or focus away from it. You can't line it up in an orderly fashion," Pax murmured soothingly as he held her hand.

"I will get him for his savage behavior. He won't hold my cupids hostage and get away with it," she said, drawing on her welding gloves. "There is no way love has anything to do with this."

"You've cloaked your powers, Harmony," Pax noted quietly. "Avoided and disguised them because you were hurt so badly. But love isn't reasonable and it will surface. If love is meant to happen between you and Jonah, it will."

"No," she said firmly. "We're not talking about love, Pax. We're talking about dislike and teaching Jonah a lesson."

The CB crackled and June's husky voice purred, "Jonah, is that you? I've got your favorite peach pie baking in the oven."

"Pax, I've got to get back to work. Will you see that the crates outside are mailed to my customers?" Harmony asked airily before she clicked off the CB and strode off to battle Therapy. When she was more calm, she would return to making cupid weather vanes. With the women of Fort Benton anxious for their orders, she would have a busy season. She would be lucky if she managed to fill the stores' orders for shipping by Christmas. But hard work squelched her thinking-about-Jonah-time and that was good.

He was a dip in her smooth-flowing road. A pock on her emotions, a— She looked down at Therapy's horn, captured tightly in her fingers. There were times when nice didn't pay, and this was one of them. Jonah had to pay for loving her so sweetly, then showing his skunkly self. She couldn't let him get away with his hit-and-run techniques, with interfering with her carefully planned life, with making her explode nor with taking her where she had never been before.

She held Therapy's horn tightly. Jonah needed a lesson about playing tour guide with her passions.

Her body clenched intimately and she refused to spend one more heartbeat imaging how he had looked filling her, riding high and magnificent on passion that she had matched.

It was *her* heart, she thought sadly. Even if he were experiencing his own traumas, he really shouldn't have done that to her deepest most-protected heart and soul.

That afternoon, Jonah looked at the pitchfork quivering, the sharp tines sunken into the wood.

He had been working furiously, pushing away the child's crying, forcing the barn into quiet and fighting what was within him. He couldn't bear to think about Grace wanting her doll—he'd never given her what she wanted so much.... Then the pitchfork hurled itself through the barn's shadows and stuck into the weathered boards.

Not that Shrimp was any help as a listening companion. Shorty Jones had called from Fort Benton with the news that Shrimp had carried her sleeping rug to Shep's statue. Shorty would see that Shrimp was well fed, but she wasn't responding to her name lately. Jonah had informed him that lately Shrimp liked being called Elizabeth. She had carried a magazine to him; the front cover was filled with photos of Elizabeth Taylor. Shrimp had plopped her paw on Elizabeth's beautiful face, claiming the name for her own.

Jonah ran his hand over his jaw, then gripped the old buggy's seat. Tucked in the barn against the elements, the buggy had been his father's pride and Jonah had carried on the tradition of polishing and keeping it primed.

Now he gripped it for a lifeline and the fringed top quivered with the force of his emotions. The cupids were getting to him.

The little bushwhackers and the lack of sleep, his body humming to return to Harmony's soft one, and the child crying made him want to run off into a Charles Russell Western painting.

He missed Harmony. Anything could set him off, triggering images of soft tawny eyes, her rosebud mouth, the surprised gasp as he filled her. No one had touched her before, not really, and she was his now....

He did not want Harmony Davis in his life. She had weird ideas and had him jumping from the moment she turned on her CB this past week. She'd led an attack on him, on the Fargo ranch, infesting it with cooing women and men determined to get what their sweethearts wanted. He wondered if there was a law stopping women from using CB's; they already monopolized his telephone's party line. "Cupids," Jonah muttered, walking out of the barn.

In the sunlight he was attacked by smirking, gleaming copper cupids.

And June. He saw her car now, and she was rushing toward him. Her eyes lit up when she saw him—hard green eyes, devouring him, her body throbbing with heat for his. He caught a flashing image of what she wanted to do to him and fear trickled up his neck.

Jonah swallowed and backed against the side of the barn as June batted her heavily mascaraed lashes up at him. When he really wanted to run from her, he nodded politely. "June."

"Why, Jonah. I heard about the cupids. I love them . . . I really do.... I didn't know you were getting ready to... to date again after so many years," she cooed, her gaze running hungrily down and up his body. "You should have told me."

Jonah blinked. He'd rather have an hourly CB showdown with Harmony, or wear cupid undershorts, than to face June even once in his lifetime. He inched to one side and she sidled closer to him, pinning him to the barn with the rather pointy tips of her breasts. He stood very still, stuck to the barn with June's distinctive twin cones, and knew instantly how much care she had taken to choose and pad her underwear. She'd searched through stores and catalogs for months for the right push-up, pointy look that she thought men liked.

He thought about Harmony's round breasts with their rose-bud tips. They were soft and sweet against him. She'd ruined him, he thought grimly, then caught a fresh mind blast of June's plans for him.

June was not getting her hands on any part of him. An image of Harmony stroking Therapy's horn zipped by him and Jonah sensed his guilt, as though he'd been unfaithful. June hadn't laid a hand on him and she wasn't going to, either.

He gripped her upper arms to remove her from his path, to get an object between them . . . like a wall or field or a mountain. Then June launched herself at him, locking her arms around his neck, and off-balance, Jonah shot one hand out to brace against the wall and the other on June's waist to protect her from falling. "Oh, Jonah . . ." she simpered immediately.

There should be a law against pointy bras, Jonah decided grimly as June clung tighter to him.

The air stilled and he caught a scent, lighter, more fragile than the woman in his arms.

Pain . . . deep riveting pain, like a heart torn apart, and crystal tears spilling from wounded amber eyes. . . . Harmony! Harmony was behind him. . . .

He tried to ease himself away from June, to turn to the woman who was now mounting her horse to run—

The image of Jonah scooping June against him, bracing his weight against the barn, tore open Harmony's patched heart.

Though she wasn't a horsewoman, she urged Pax's mare to race, carrying her away from Jonah.

Harmony leaned forward in the saddle, wiping her tears away with her hand and locking her body to the mare's. Each rapid heartbeat ripped more pain into her, or was it the pounding hoofbeats?

She had given her heart, her life, to him.

She would be lying to herself if she didn't admit that she loved Jonah Fargo.

Thundering hoofbeats filled the bright April morning. Too many hoofbeats for one horse. Harmony glanced over her shoulder, brushed away a strand of hair and saw Jonah riding after her, his dark face as grim as any outlaw's. A part of the

land, of the tough men who had settled it, Jonah looked as
though nothing would stop him.

She couldn't let him see her pain . . . not now, when pieces of
her were lying on the plains . . . when she was too vulnerable. . . .

She concentrated on the mare, sending her fear into the reins
and to the horse who understood.

Jonah? Fear surged through her—not her emotions, but another's. *Jonah?*

His fear for her surged around her, fueling her pain.

She glanced at a sign, a tree and then a field and knew that
she'd circled the Fargo property. Jonah's house lay in the afternoon shadows, and she urged the mare over a knoll and toward safety. All she needed was a moment before he arrived—
if he decided to make the circle back to his ranch. She'd paste
her emotions into a cement wall that Jonah could not pene-
trate.

Harmony dismounted and ran into the house, locking the
door. She splashed water on her face, drying it, and trying to
pull the tiny strips of her emotions into line before seeing Jonah.

She closed her eyes. He'd never circle back, and for the moment she was safe. Her head throbbed, she ached in her soul
and her heart, and he wouldn't see her this way. . . .

In a few minutes she'd be fine . . . she'd be back to calm, capable Harmony; she'd find a way to explain her actions. . . .

Jonah?

"If you think a locked door is keeping me from you, guess
again," he stated a heartbeat before the door crashed open, the
upper hinge tearing free from the force of Jonah's shoulder.

Harmony gripped the kitchen counter with both hands and
shook; she concentrated on the dish hurling through the air at
Jonah. He caught it just as thunder crashed in the room and a
bolt of lightning lashed between them.

So he was angry now, was he? So was she. . . . Smoke boiled
from the stove, though there were no flames, and the dinosaur
teeth began rattling on the table.

Several bottles exploded and the scent of his after-shave filled
the wind-whipped room.

"You're crying," he said suddenly, very quietly, and the turbulence in the house eased.

"No. Really?" she asked mockingly as tears slid freely down her cheeks and she dashed them away. Trust Jonah to change his mood quickly, leaving her with a magnificent, unused mad aura. The floorboards seemed to bounce beneath her feet—or was that due to Jonah's weight as he crossed the room to her and jerked her into his arms, burying his face in her hair?

His heart thudded against her, pounding his fear for her safety into her senses.

Harmony stood very still in his arms, her body tense and shaking. She read the images of June's breasts against him, more firm and defined than her own softness. "Let me go, Mr. Fargo."

She refused to fight him, to give him the pleasure of subduing her easily. She'd been rejected before; she should have known better. "I said, let me go," she stated, hating the tearful tremor in her voice. She wanted her raging anger back—she'd flatten Jonah's lesser powers and walk out of his life.

Darn...how like him to send her emotions shifting, needing his cuddling and cherishing....

Jonah cradled her closer, easing her body against his as though he wanted to make her a part of himself...to keep her safe. "Don't cry, Harmony," he was saying unevenly, a deep shudder moving through his body. "Please don't cry."

She wasn't crying...she wasn't. Not for a buckaroo whom she had claimed as her own—who had done fantastic, memorable claiming of his own, and now was roaming the range romancing other women. She hated him fiercely then, the images of June's pointy breast impressions slashing at her. Oh, fine. Every centimeter of her broken heart came welling up her throat to cry, "You made love to me. Don't deny it. You've certainly gotten bored quick. Or aren't I enough?"

He caught her head gently in the cradle of his hand, keeping her locked to him with the other. "Harmony... Harmony...listen to me. Don't—"

"Don't? Don't what?" She stared up at him through her tears and found Jonah's worried expression. Fine, let him be worried. She was shattering. Since she'd met him, she'd been either ecstatic, angry, or weepy. With Jonah there was no easygoing relationship, and now he had cradled another woman against him, held her body in his arms, and... She swiped away tears—evidence of her bleeding heart. He certainly had quick moves for a man who had thoroughly welded himself to her.

She pushed her hands against his shoulders and the bells on her wrist tinkled eerily. She rattled them beneath his nose. "Do you know why I wear these? To keep me from people like you— disaster people, trouble people, illogical, dark, moody auras, who aren't sensitive in the least—"

She looked at his lips. She had to know.... Then she locked her hands to his ears and pulled his lips against hers. Though she tasted the salt of her tears, she didn't taste another woman. "Put me down," Harmony ordered shakily.

Good. Jonah looked stunned. She had pulled out her little poleax and whacked him—Mr. Quick Moves Fargo who left her hanging in the middle of a really good storm fit. She concentrated on the hot sauce bottle on the kitchen counter and it shattered satisfyingly. Though her powers weren't strong in that area, she had accomplished her threat.

Jonah didn't look away or seem startled; he was concentrating on her. She sniffed, unsettled with the immediate knowledge that when Jonah focused on her, nothing else mattered to him.

She hadn't asked for the comfort of his arms around her. She squirmed slightly and knew that Jonah would hold safe anything he wished.

"Let you go after that nightmare ride? No," he said firmly and lifted her in his arms. "I'm holding you until we both settle down. You could have been hurt. Don't you realize that ride was dangerous? That field is filled with gopher holes... the mare could have gone down...."

"There will be none of this," Harmony stated with another sniff as Jonah sank into the couch, holding her on his lap. This man was exhausting, draining her emotions. Or was it the lack of sleep and her psyche on overdrive because of him? "I just came to get my cupids... that's all. I care less about disgusting clinch scenes involving you and June."

"I do. She scares me." Jonah smoothed her curls with his cheek and cuddled her against him. "I can hear your heart pounding," he whispered unevenly against her hair.

"So what?" She breathed sharply, realizing that Jonah was trying to understand, his mind searching her reactions to him. She was calmer now, leaping into the swift current of his thoughts. He thought she cared for him...that he had hurt her and he feared he would say the wrong thing. He'd never seen anything so frightening as her racing over the countryside, an unskilled city woman with a pretty backside that should be held and caressed by a man regularly.

When she could ride better, he'd like to take her out to his favorite dinosaur dig. Not many women appreciated dinosaur finds, but Harmony was a sensitive woman. She'd fit in his sleeping bag, cute as a—

Trust Jonah not to keep their argument on a safe level or notice her threat and first-accomplished shattering, breaking the hot sauce bottle.

"Don't you think about making love to me now, Jonah Fargo," she stated darkly, glaring at him. "If you were a sensible man—which you are not—you would realize that *we* are not pleased. Lovemaking is not on my schedule with you. Not even a kiss. Not one."

"No...wouldn't think about it, rosebud," he said very quietly, gathering her softening body closer to his. "I'd just do it naturally."

"Not now, Jonah. Not ever again. I've learned my lesson about trusting lanky Montana buckaroos," she said unevenly, placing her elbow firmly into the spot on his chest that had touched June's breasts.

"I like soft warm women with round curves," Jonah said huskily, smoothing her thighs gently.

She clamped her thighs together tightly and Jonah's open hand settled on her stomach. *A claiming.* His every touch on her was a claiming, yet he had embraced the infamous peach pie maker.

"I don't make peach pies and you are not a nice man."

Darn. Why did her bones and flesh seem to turn so easily in his direction? she lamented as Jonah began kissing the tears from her damp lashes. "You scared me," he admitted shakily, stroking her taut neck and shoulders. "Don't do that again. Ever."

"So I'm not a skilled rider. But you don't have to say anything about my bottom bouncing in the saddle," she whispered back.

"Did I say that?" he asked with a slight, whimsical smile. "I did notice that it was real cute—high up there in the air...off the saddle—real soft-like...just a bit of jiggle going on beneath your jeans when you bounced."

"I do not jiggle or bounce. Don't say intimate things like that when we're having summit talks. Try to keep on the subject at hand. It's easy to read you, Jonah Fargo. Sure...talk this way...hold me here, prisoner on your lap, like you're holding my cupids—I just came by to make arrangements to buy them from you. By the way, I didn't come to check on your latest...latest—" She swallowed and licked at the tear that had collected at the corner of her mouth.

Jonah kissed that sensitive spot and gathered her closer, placing her head on his shoulder. "Let's sit like this for a while and mull this problem...what has stirred you, rosebud."

The problem was she loved him and she'd overreacted instantly. She should have carried on a normal, light conversation with Jonah and the infamous June. She should have offered him a reasonable amount of money for cupid ransom. But she hadn't done those things and he'd run her down, captured her and now wanted to pry the gory, heartbreaking details from her. He couldn't have them; she refused to have her emotions dissected. "I have to go now...a busy day, Jonah. Customers. Work on Therapy. Book work...accounts...ordering new copper sheets, you know," she protested as Jonah eased back and tucked her damp face against his throat. Her fingers tightened on his shirt and his heart pounded heavily beneath her cheek.

"That Therapy monster appeals to me for some reason.... Now tell me why you ran from me," he said after she'd dried her eyes on his shirt collar.

The scene of June in his arms slashed through her again.

"She's got strange underwear," Jonah stated ominously, his mind cruising through images and open to her probes. He didn't like June touching him at all; his loving belonged to his sweet little rosebud. Harmony sat very still, curled upon Jonah's hard lap, as she tapped into his thoughts. He'd plan something rash because June wasn't choosing his loving moments for him and she wasn't getting that close to him again, either.... June would be the perfect revenge for Lucky.

Jonah's thoughts settled into an even hum. He had what he wanted sitting right in his arms. If he could just get her into his bed, he'd show her with his body that she was special, a part of him now.

Harmony swallowed. "Special isn't a very—"

She clamped her lips closed. She would not tell Jonah that he was far past the special mark on her scale of heart mates.

"Women are hard to understand," he began in a thoughtful, Western wisdom tone as he kissed her temple. "You're too emotional and get all the wrong readings from nothing."

"'Emotional?'" she repeated in an outraged tone. "*I love you, you jerk,*" she shot back at him, the statement hovering in the air; she realized instantly that her frustration with his density had caused her to speak aloud.

She tried to scoot off his lap and made it to his knee, then Jonah grabbed her thigh. He leaned forward to gather her back to him. He grunted as her elbow bumped into his ribs; they overbalanced and went down on the floor.

"This isn't where I want to be," Harmony said primly after she got her breath. Jonah's weight above her, and his thoughtful, intense expression caused her to squirm. She noted belatedly that Jonah had protected her in the fall, keeping his body tense and cradling hers until she settled gently to the floor.

She certainly couldn't afford to be gentle with him; she'd just told him she loved him.

She turned her head away—she didn't want him to see into her, not now—and spotted another pair of his boots at her eye level and tried his quick-shifting topic technique. "You should polish your boots more. The leather is drying."

"Boots..." he repeated distantly. Jonah settled comfortably upon her, trapping her legs with his, braced his weight on his elbows and caught her face with his hands. His fingers smoothed her hot cheeks, drying the tear trails. "Tell me the part about you loving me again, Harmony."

"Only you would double back to Fargo land, to this house. That was really low and calculating. You disgust me. Just disgust me," she stated hotly and began squirming with all her might to dislodge him.

Jonah chose not to be dislodged; his hand spanned her hip, claiming her firmly and heating her through the layers of clothing. He studied her intently, tracing her tangled hair, her tear-filled eyes and her trembling lips. Because she was aghast with her admission, spoken aloud and surprising herself, Harmony shivered.

She couldn't love him.

She'd given herself to him in the deepest way and he'd betrayed her for a peach pie baker with a cone bra.

Then Jonah slowly settled his face into the cove of her throat— Oh, no! Why did he have to go for that vulnerable spot? She could have refused him if he'd placed his lips anywhere else but at the base of her throat. If he just hadn't seemed so vulnerable himself. If he—

"Because this is where I can feel your heart against my cheek and your pulse beneath my lips. Feels like a pretty little bird with wild fluttering wings . . . one that was hurt," he murmured gently. "I'm sorry you were hurt, rosebud."

"Hurt? Me? No . . . I wasn't . . ." But she was shattered, shot through the heart. Worst of all, she'd told him she loved him. She'd spread her pride before him. She couldn't allow him to actually believe that . . . that she ached as though a part of her had been torn away. "Get off me, Jonah."

He ignored her, his thumbs caressing her cheeks, following the tear trails. "You really came over here to rescue your cupids? Or did you miss me?"

"Miss you? Ha. That will be the day."

But Jonah was thinking how sweet she was . . . how ripe and sweet she felt beneath him. Jonah thought she looked cuter than a newborn calf in a spring meadow. Prettier than little bunny rabbits snuggled together under a perky-fresh daisy. Better than a sunflower opening to catch the sunlight or a frisky colt playing with a butterfly. Better than the dawn catching jewels on the dew of a spider's web. Tastier than a wild berry pie.

Harmony inhaled, assailed by his thoughts, which were stronger than she remembered. His sending powers were developing, growing. He was too deep in his thoughts to be sensitive to hers. Jonah had probably thought the same thing about other women. *She* would not be his 'sweet and ripe' anything ever again. She was out for revenge, deadly in her purpose to bring him to his knees—once her cupids were safe. They were the only—repeat, only—reason she'd come to his ranch. "That's exactly why. To rescue my orphans—er...my cupids. How much?"

"I'll think it over," he said quietly, then lowered his lips to hers. "You think about this."

Oh, no... She would remember thinking later.

Oh, yes, rosebud...

Later that night, when he could trust himself to ride to the knoll overlooking Harmony's cabin, Jonah leaned against a tree and listened to her wind chimes.

He wanted to walk down the knoll and—what?

After Harmony had responded so sweetly, so hungrily to his kiss, she'd eased free of his weight and frowned at his chest. "Stay away from me, Fargo," she had said in a quiet, low tone. Then she'd walked out the battered door, her head held high and her shoulders straight.

He'd hurt her badly.

Harmony was a fierce, wildly loving woman and a sweet rosebud wrapped up in one volatile package. When he'd caught her at her circle-back-and-hide act, she'd exploded right in front of him. For just a second, he thought the room was filled with a summer storm, complete with thunder and lightning. The old stove chimney had tilted and briefly smoke had boiled into the room. Bottles had dropped and broken with the force of his breaking down the door—

Jonah grimaced. At that moment, leaping off his mare at a run into the house, he'd known that no door would keep him from Harmony; she was his. He hadn't tried the lock because he'd known she had turned it—how had he known?

"Reasonable," he answered his question, then added "You scared her chasing her like that—how was she supposed to act?"

With the soft musical chimes sounding in the wind and the moon overhead, Jonah regretted that he had hurt her.

He'd been too tangled in his troubles—lack of sleep, the gnawing suspicion that he'd kept Grace's doll overlong. A cold emptiness moved inside him, and he knew that Harmony's warmth alone could warm him.

He closed his eyes again, reliving the fear that she would fall from the mare, that he would never be able to tell her the things that were on his mind...such as the pleasure he knew just looking at her, tilting her temper just a bit.

Impressions circled him when he thought about Harmony's past. Then he knew that few people had known the emotional woman beneath Harmony's smooth walls. Pax had said she was a calm woman.

She'd been hurt before and deeply; he'd sensed that when he held her, felt her tears on his throat.

He shouldn't have let her get to him, to get caught in the cross fires of his shifting mind. Jonah sucked on a wheat stalk and studied the moon.

She was a proud woman. *"I love you, you jerk,"* she'd said.

Jonah shook his head and his mare nickered softly to him. Funny way for a woman to say a thing like that. He shrugged. Maybe he was a jerk.

Jonah swallowed the emotion tightening his throat. He'd seen into her...read her thoughts. Or was it her tears and her expression? She was right. He should have called after loving her. He should have told her that he was thinking of her...keeping her close when he thought he was losing his mind and when he was catching images from people he'd known all of his life. When he was near them, sensations from other people lurched at him like river snags. He received colorful pictures if he focused on that person.

The church matron had gloated; she had done well with her whipping cream sensual expedition. Her husband, at seventy-plus, had responded nicely. Their marriage had not lost anything, but the years had made it stronger and my, my, how pleased Elmer was with himself, how his eyes sparkled and she was feeling a bit frisky herself.

Jonah threw the wheat stalk away abruptly.

He didn't have psychic abilities; he did have a slanting mind. He was just bone tired and aching for the child that kept cry-

ing. He admitted to the emptiness of not having a child in his
life.

He'd had a daughter and wasn't ready to give up Grace's
doll, his link to her. Though he didn't believe Harmony's
mental malarkey, he had deep feelings for her. More than deep.

She loved him. How could a man not notice a thing like that?

Was he so far-gone that he didn't know the tenderness a
woman could feel? *I love you, you jerk....*

At two o'clock in the morning, Jonah settled down by Shep's
statue. He carefully skinned and deboned a plate of fried
chicken for Shrimp.

The peace gift bought him complete attention when Shrimp
finished the slivers and lay down beside him. She placed her
head on his lap and considered the sweeping Missouri River as
he petted her.

In Shrimp-Elizabeth's opinion, if a woman said she loved a
jerk, that no-good had better make himself appealing—if that
jerk wanted to keep whatever depleted tenderness the woman
felt for him...even if he really didn't deserve that tenderness...the jerk really should change his current "M.O."—
method of operation. Obviously Shrimp had been talking to
several policemen lately.

"I'm some love god, huh?" Jonah muttered, as a whimsical
memory swirled around him. Had they made love the night
he'd fallen asleep at her house? Was that why she was so familiar to him, a part of him before lovemaking the second time?

Lovemaking wasn't the correct word; his feelings for Harmony went deeper, as if they were melded together by the
flames enclosing them.

Shrimp-Elizabeth sighed and looked up at Shep's magnificent collie statue. Though the chicken treat was nice, everyone
in town was serving her goodies and telling her their problems
at the odd hours. She was exhausted from all the companionship and asked that Jonah return home. He needed work on his
Harmony problem. Shrimp-Elizabeth was certain that he would
be installed back on his love-god perch in no time if—

"If?" Jonah prompted, realizing he'd been concentrating on
Shrimp-Elizabeth intently.

But Shrimp-Elizabeth was staring longingly at Shep.

Nine

The first thing Harmony noticed when she saw Jonah walking down Fort Benton's historic Front Street was his aura. Usually auras were vague and "read" by colors and impressions, but Jonah's was distinct. It wasn't the ordinary multicolored mist tipped in sparks or streamers. It stuck out from his battered black hat, as distinct as Therapy's horn. She didn't trust her reading of it; after a closer look, she saw cheery little ribbon streamers reaching toward her. She gripped the shipping carton in her arms tightly; though Jonah's vital energy was focused on her, she wanted nothing to do with that buckaroo and his bricklike mind.

Western hats with their broad brims made it very difficult to read expressions, but Jonah's blue eyes locked on her. From the price tag swinging under his arm, he'd purchased a new blue shirt, his jeans were stiffly new and he'd attempted to polish his scuffed boots. There was no way she could miss that Jonah had her on his mind, psychic abilities or not. As he swept toward her, he kept those blue lasering eyes on her while his tentacle streamers quivered toward her.

Then he saw the little girl holding her ragged doll close and shyly hugging her mother's leg. Jonah stopped, his expression

changing into tenderness and longing. Anyone could see that
he was deeply affected as he crouched beside the six year-old
girl and spoke quietly to her. When he stood, he took out his
worn wallet and gave the woman money. He watched as the
mother and daughter entered the grocery store.

Of course she loved Jonah Fargo. But why did she have to
admit it to him? she wondered desperately. Why did she just
have to blurt it out like a hot water kettle flipping its pressure
valve?

He did not fit her prespecifications for a relationship.

She hugged the carton of cupid wind chimes to be shipped to
Seattle. Just three days after her damning admission that she
loved him, Jonah—a tall, lean tough cowboy—was wrapped in
a cheery aura with tiny tentaclelike ribbons that were reaching
out for her.

Aura reading was another of her psychic weaknesses, but
today Jonah's was neon bright.

Now, in the first week of June, the impression that Jonah
wanted to make amends and reclaim his love-god status was so
strong that Harmony took a step backward. She noted that
people came out of their stores in Jonah's wake. Their minds
hummed busily as they watched him.

*When a man exuded that much animal magnetism and strode
toward the desired lady object of his thoughts, people were
certain to notice.*

Sunlight glistened around him, his ribbon aura curling from
him toward her. Harmony stepped backward and bumped into
Lucky, whose arms closed around her, steadying her briefly.
Lucky released her quickly when Jonah loomed over them.

Over her head, the two men exchanged grim, meaningful
stares as though debating territorial rights. Harmony blinked
disbelievingly. Jonah and Lucky were locked in eye combat
over the possession of one Harmony Davis; they were making
mental growling noises and calling each other "sweetheart," in
the true old West tradition. Jonah was thinking something really odd—that Lucky better tell the other "girls" that Harmony was wearing a big Fargo brand. Harmony remembered
a Western movie in which the cowboys called other men
"girls." Lucky was thinking that, *sweetheart, the roundup ain't
over 'til it's over.*

She wanted to drop the carton on their boots. *She* had made her choice and the matter was not up for discussion. *She* also enjoyed Lucky's charming personality and his savvy fashion sense.

Then Lucky looked away, like a gunfighter who wanted to live, and Jonah smiled down at Harmony. He eased the heavy carton from her arms. "Pretty day, isn't it?"

Lucky frowned warily. "Did I just see you smile, Fargo?"

Harmony backed away a step, fogged by Jonah's grim intention to be acceptable to her. When he continued smiling down at her, the sunlight caught his teeth and they flashed, blinding her. She blinked and shivered and studied the clear blue depths of his eyes.

Jonah Fargo had courting and claiming on his mind. He had plans to have her share his sleeping bag and camp out at the dinosaur dig before winter arrived. He had just a few months to restore himself to the status of her love god.... And he had big plans for his Christmas present and for hers.

But the custom cutters would be circling the area in August, when it was harvest time for wheat. Touring the countryside from Kansas to Montana, the professional wheat harvesting crews drove fancy trucks and swarmed into town. One look at Harmony and the way her amber eyes lit up and her blond-coppery hair frilled out wildly in the wind, just asking for a man's hand to tame it, and the unmarried custom cutters would be— Jonah would have to step up his pace and try to be appealing. *How?* he wondered, and Harmony thought of ways to tell him that she wasn't on his calendar. Right now the custom cutters sounded interesting.

They might appreciate her cupids. *They* might not think her hair was messy and needed taming. She blew away a spiraling curl from her hot cheek.

She was cute in a snit, Jonah was thinking, his smile down at her tender.

Snit? Me in a snit? Never! Harmony smiled blandly, refusing to let Jonah into her mad parlor. There were lots of reasons she was in a possible...snit...and Jonah was at the bottom of all of them.

"Where do you want this carton?" Jonah asked, glancing over her head at Lucky. The question to her wasn't pleasant; it was a threat to Lucky.

"I—I," she stammered, looking up at Lucky for help and found him smiling sadly.

While Lucky really wanted her companionship and interesting discussions about his designer talent, he couldn't ignore the code of the West. Fargo had placed his brand on Harmony and Lucky wasn't trespassing...unless things didn't work out with Fargo...and there was no reason they should, because Fargo was an ornery cuss. Lucky would just bide his time and wait for Harmony to fall into his hands naturally as most women did. Except June Fields; she'd been running from him for years. June needed help choosing her clothes and her underwear; she needed less point and less flash to frame her assets.

"Fargo. Harmony," Lucky said in that wise, traditional Western drawl. Then he touched the brim of his Western hat in an *adios* and walked toward Shep's statue. Jonah continued watching him as Shrimp-Elizabeth invited the cowboy into her parlor. It was time for a heart-to-heart chat about June Fields.

"Why did you do that?" Harmony demanded. "You ran him off." She turned back to Jonah, who was studying the sunlight shimmering on her hair, piled high on top of her head.

He slowly looked at her face, taking in her features, and found the tiny pulse at the base of her throat. Then his gaze skimmed down her light pink sweater, touched the cupid necklace and followed her jeans to lock onto her work boots. His sensual thoughts dropped into Harmony's mind and she caught how much he liked her strong thighs before his mind moved on. "Been working on Therapy lately?" he asked in a sensual drawl that went straight to the hairs at the nape of her neck, lifting them.

Her midnight welding hours weren't of his concern. She parted her lips to tell him so and blinked, swirling amid enjoyable sensations.

His aura's happy, little sunlit ribbons gently wrapped around her, trickling around the round lines of her body with familiarity and tugging her toward him. His thoughts dropped in on her. Jonah was in a really good mood; he felt as if he were standing on Front Street with his best girl. *She loved him. She had told him so and his little prairie dew-dipped rosebud wasn't one to toss things like that out freely. He promised to improve the "jerk" part of her love statement to "honey," "lover," "darling" or whatever Harmony wanted.*

Harmony locked her work boots onto the historic street's concrete sidewalk and fought her body's trembling. She really liked those gentle, stroking ribbons, smoothing her body. Jonah's aura was the first to touch her like a lover. However, because she was still miffed with him, she refused to let her aura do likewise. "I'd like my cupids back, please," she said firmly. "I don't want to give anyone the wrong idea. I wanted to pay you back for saving my life—"

"I miss you, rosebud," he said in a low intimate tone that curled her insides and warmed her in places that only Jonah had touched. All of his aura's little ribbons smoothed her up and down, caressingly. They played in the froth of curls over her head.

Harmony's bells jingled as she lifted her hand to smooth her hair. She was certain her topnotch of curls was dancing with her body's shivering as Jonah grinned at her. Trust him to produce her first aura-feel-caress.

He had a thousand-watt, love-god grin, unfair at the moment because she hadn't realized how powerful Jonah could be when he tried. Twin little curving bits of sunlight slid from him to stroke her hair with a lover's touch.

She said she loves me . . . all I have to do is be nice . . . take it easy . . . and—

"You jerk," she said tightly, grabbing her carton of cupid wind chimes from him. "You're not getting these."

He raised one finger to lightly tap the hair on top of her head and studied the movement as though he were making a scientific experiment. "You need riding lessons. Bet you were sore from that saddle pounding your backside. Better let me teach you how to grip with your thighs and feel the horse roll under you. It's a rhythm thing."

Harmony sniffed. She'd ached after attaching her cupids to his rooftops and later when she'd pitted herself against him. Her knowledge was sufficient about rhythm things and gripping them with her thighs. One of Jonah's stealthy little ribbon-feelers was slipping under her pink sweater now. He really appreciated her sensible underwear and round curves. She was just ripe and sweet as a canned peach from her curly topknot down to her work boots. She realized suddenly that she was holding her breath and her body was arching, responding to the caressing motions of his aura.

"Your brother thinks you're quiet, organized and calm. He's wrong," Jonah stated as her body began picking up the crashing heat waves from his. The warm ribbon gently closed around her nipple, flicking the end just as Jonah had done with the tip of his tongue.

Another gentle, pleasing, tentacle ribbon eased down the rounded line of her hip, curved around her, then eased upward to slide down inside her jeans. It gently stroked her femininity, lovingly, cherishing her.

Jonah was thinking about how flushed she was and that she was his little sweetheart and that if he worked on improving his jerk image, home on the range wouldn't be so lonely this Christmas.

She took a step backward. Jonah in a whimsical, out-to-get-her mood was frightening. "I...I have to be going. Sorry I can't spend time chatting with you."

"Shrimp has left me," he said in a lonely, deserted tone that cruised straight to her sympathetic nerves and lifted their antennae to full quiver.

"She'll be back," she murmured, unable to block her caring, soothing tendencies.

"I've got something to show you," he offered in a low husky drawl that dried her throat. Then he bent to kiss the fast-beating pulse in her throat. Every tiny warm caressing Jonah-aura-ribbon gathered her to him gently.

If his darn little feelers would release her, stop caressing her so gently and sweetly, she'd run.

She steeled herself against Jonah's darkened blue eyes, the heady warmth of his body and pushed his sunlit invisible ribbons away with all her psychic might. In another minute, she'd repeat her "I love you" and melt against him. With Jonah's unpredictable nature, she surrendered the field—Fort Benton's historic Front Street—and kept her pride.

* * *

Lucky studied the peach pies cooling on Jonah's table. He glanced at Jonah. He was frowning at the pies, and dusting flour from the bath towel he wore as an apron. Lucky sank his hands in the soapy dishwater and began scrubbing. "It's a poor world when a guy has to get himself in the right again by helping bake pies on a Friday evening. I'll barely have time to fix up for the dance," Lucky muttered. "When we put these cupids up, I was just helping Harmony thank you...to pay you back for saving her life. Shoot. I'd help you take them down now, if you asked, Fargo. But oh, no...you wanted me to help you bake peach pies."

Jonah touched the button on the fan; it began pushing the layers of smoke out the open window. "Who would know that pies boil over?" he muttered. "I could see from the recipe book that pie baking was a two-man job, Lucky. I appreciate you delivering and putting on my roof, but it wasn't enough for the desecration damage. And I'm keeping those cupids."

"What about June-bug?" Lucky asked softly. "If these pies are for Harmony, then June is not yours, right?"

Jonah probed the burnt crusts critically, then carefully sprinkled sugar over the worst places. "Never was."

"Good. I never saw a woman weld like Harmony. Janice said that Harmony is working on a metal monster thing with a horn. Seems she calls it Therapy."

Jonah turned slowly to him. "Don't worry about Harmony's welding projects," he warned. "You just think about getting back the tools you've borrowed from me over the years. I'm going back to wheat ranching."

But Lucky was drying his hands, his Western boots clumping across the floor to study the stacks of books on Jonah's coffee table. "Paranormal? Mystical?" he asked, picking up and studying the book titles. "Weird stuff."

Jonah tried an experiment—a whimsical investment in nonsense that he didn't believe. He concentrated on Lucky's thoughts and the cowboy frowned, turning to him. "Did you say something, Jonah?"

Burnt-peach-pie-scented smoke swirled in the room between them and Jonah felt the hairs at the back of his neck lift slightly. "No," he said quietly, thinking that Lucky should lasso June. Jonah shook his head; it wasn't possible that Lucky could understand his thoughts. "Didn't say a word."

"Hmm. I got the feeling that you were trying to...." He replaced the psychic book he'd been flipping through and glanced at Jonah with a puzzled expression. "Funny. I was just thinking that you thought I ought to finally corral June.... Never mind. I always thought that someday June and I would eventually get around to each other."

After Lucky had gone, Jonah sat and stared at the books. He didn't believe in ESP, telepathy, clairvoyance or any of the other psychic phenomena.

He pushed his fingers through his hair, noted the new price tag beneath his arm and ripped it away. Clothes had never made a difference to him, but he didn't want Harmony to be ashamed of him as a potential ... what? He was just losing his mind and was dopey over a woman who believed in the paranormal. Harmony said he had "abilities." He didn't understand "powers" and "abilities" and he sure as shootin' didn't want them.

Before Harmony explained, how did he know she'd been touched by a man named Mark?

Why did he feel as though he were holding a part of his daughter by holding that old doll?

Why was he starting to sense—"read," the books called it— what other people were thinking?

When he picked Harmony out of the blizzard, how did Harmony know about his plans for June?

What was all that business before Christmas when he imagined Harmony in a black negligee? Jonah stopped worrying and concentrated on that memory. Then he skipped to the first time he'd made love with Harmony—when he was asleep. "Dreams," he muttered. "Just dreams."

The tiny kitten that he'd gotten from Myrtle Hanks meowed and began to claw its way up his jean leg. The kitten's tawny fur reminded him of Harmony's amber eyes, and—Jonah stood and cuddled the kitten close to his cheek. She licked his skin and rubbed against him, just as Harmony had done.

"Well...may as well take our peach pie and go on our way," he said to the kitten. "You have a job to do, kitty. Buy me some points with Harmony. I've lost a few, and from the looks of things, I need all the help I can get."

"Jonah baked a peach pie for you? Jonah?" Pax's laughter filled the cabin. He collapsed into Harmony's kitchen chair and tried unsuccessfully to stop laughing.

She tossed a tea towel at him and Pax used it to swipe away the tears on his cheeks. He pointed at the burned pie, started to say something, then erupted in laughter again.

Harmony clumped her work boots in a steady rhythm and waited tensely for him to finish. "Jonah also brought me Amber."

"Amber?"

"A beautiful little kitten. She's sleeping now, but Jonah said she reminded him of me. Stop laughing, Pax. You didn't have Jonah standing on your porch and looking like a lost little boy. He was so proud of his peach pie, his first attempt. When he gave me Amber, he was so shy. It was all I could do not to hug him."

"You didn't eat that missing piece, did you?" Pax asked with a grin. "And by the way, you're the only person I know who might see Jonah as having little-boy endowments. That new mustache he's sporting makes him seem more weathered."

"Don't pick on his mustache. He's developing his new look. He's trying new things and that's important. He was so eager for me to taste his handiwork. How could I refuse?"

"I would have. Come on, Harmony. Give up and admit that you recognized him as your other half as soon as you met him. Jonah doesn't fit your prespecifications for a relationship, but you're stuck with that cowboy."

Harmony considered the missing piece of pie and how much water she had drunk to remove the aftertaste. She refused to lay any tidbits beneath Pax's nose. Waiting for Jonah in the three weeks, one day, twelve hours and fifty-four seconds since they'd made love had taught her a lesson. While she had ached for him desperately, he was taking his time. No man in love would act as Jonah had done, leaving his bonded mate alone and aching—her telephone and CB were at his beck and call...just one little call. Then she had humiliated herself in his arms. "I am *not* stuck with him. I refuse to be hurt further. I sent him home, of course."

"Oh, right. Of course."

The next morning, Harmony breezed by the barbershop where Jonah was getting his hair trimmed. In midstride, she tensed and caught the full blast of his focus on her backside. His thoughts swished out of the barbershop and latched on to her. His lap was very empty, and he liked holding her on it. She tried not to let her hips sway while walking hurriedly to the drugstore.

His need to hold her was frightening; she was a thirty-nine-year-old career woman who had always kept her life unencumbered with troublesome people, and Jonah was proven, grade-A trouble.

Now here she was, fairly running down the street in her work boots from a man who wanted to cuddle her. Every five-foot-eight, athletic, Amazon inch of her.

She was hurriedly paying for her purchases when Jonah appeared at her side. "Good morning, Harmony," he said in a deep tone that caused her to shiver.

Customers in the drugstore began to gather, watching Harmony and Jonah stealthily. Their thoughts settled into a steady, approving hum. She clutched her sack close to her chest and once again felt Jonah's little caresser feelers pet her. Her body warmed to his touch and she knew immediately when his dark blue eyes locked to hers that he wanted to kiss her. Since she'd spent the night wallowing in dreams of his kisses and bonding and mating, she was extremely susceptible to his need of her. "Have to go," she stated airily. "Busy. Very busy."

While she was too tense and anxious to be a safe thinking distance from Jonah, the alert senses of the customers caught her. Every one of them had a whimsical grin and the room hummed steadily with their thoughts. They liked Jonah and it was time someone took him to task. They hoped he'd be happy, and they liked the new coppersmith city woman, but they truly were enjoying the sparks flying between Jonah and herself. They hoped the entertainment would last a bit longer. Watching Jonah perk up with the coppersmith lady was more fun than golfing or watching tourists or going on historical digs. He looked just like his dad with that new mustache—a real lady-killer without a clue to how women wanted to snatch him. Harmony apparently couldn't resist Jonah, because once a person got past his ornery cuss facade, he was "true gold." He was just like the Fargo men before him, finding a ladylove and keeping true to her for his lifetime.

Harmony sniffed. To date, there was no reason to believe that she was Jonah's only ladylove. She probably had done the ground-breaking ceremony for others.

"She's on the run," someone whispered. Or did they think it?

"She's been dancing out of his reach for a week now," she knew someone else thought, because the store was very quiet. Too quiet. No one was speaking aloud.

Jonah reached to smooth a tendril from her temple, his fingertips lingering on her skin. "Harmony," he said simply, achingly.

She took one look at him, realized that her heart was beating for him and said firmly, "Come to dinner tonight, Jonah. Don't be late.... Ah ... you won't need to bring anything."

That evening, Harmony set the table for two, then changed her clothes several times. She'd acted impulsively, untrue to her contemplative nature, and it was Jonah's fault. She wanted everything settled in her world. She wanted regular sleeping patterns, set working hours and wanted to stop eating nervously. Or dreaming about Jonah holding her close and looking as if he'd never looked at or held anyone but her.

Harmony wanted harmony in her life. She would lay out the rules for Jonah, thus beginning a logical life....

The bottom line was that she loved Jonah Fargo, mean Montana cuss who had deserted her on the morning after their loving. She couldn't stand the lines and shadows clinging to his face, reminders of his sleepless nights. He needed her care and attention and he was getting it. She tugged a basic black sheath over her head and adjusted the hem around her thighs.

She'd mentor him on the sly; he wouldn't realize it and she'd gradually infuse the idea into him that psychic abilities didn't have to be one's life priority. A balance of relationships with others and being comfortable with one's self was extremely important. Once Jonah understood that, he'd have to release certain doubts and believe in the future. Then his life would settle into place. The mirror caught her and Harmony studied her Harmony-with-Jonah image. Long, wild hair atop flushed cheeks and luminous amber eyes—"The kitten reminds me of you—gold and shimmering . . . amber eyes . . . like a tiger."

Harmony fluffed her hair over her bare shoulders. She ran her fingers over the dress's two tiny straps and thought of the drab shapeless dresses and slacks she had preferred before meeting Jonah. This tight little number and the leopard-print dress were her "today's woman" statements—in control, a business woman at play and feminine. She'd never been a tiger woman before. She felt hot and fine. Double hot and fine when she was with Jonah. And very, very strong as an empowered woman.

While Jonah hovered around with his tantalizing little caresser feelers, Harmony had decided to become a woman of action.

Over dinner, she would keep on schedule, be gentle with him, persevering and understanding. She would keep the conversation light, yet directed and meaningful. She wouldn't let him tilt her emotions, because Jonah needed to understand the balance and give and take in the relationship she proposed. A gentle understanding, developing relationship. To release his inhibitions, she might keep his wineglass filled and the music soothing. After dinner, with the lights turned low, she'd allow him to hold her hand, and she would impart her thoughts to him. All this equating would be very gentle, very firm and scheduled.

Tonight, after her plans were in place, she would test Jonah as he had never been tried before. She would release every hot molecule of her love for him, and if he withstood the test . . . she'd treat him very gently, but honestly; she would not shield her real self from him, and truly she was a strong woman.

Jonah? She listened to the hoofbeats coming closer and ran to the window. A horse pulling a buggy crossed the moonlit road to her house.

Jonah didn't come in. He stopped the horse, slid from the covered buggy and stood there in the moonlight, looking perfectly . . . perfectly . . .

He propped his boot on a wooden spoke and looked at the cabin, willing her to come to him. She sensed that while Jonah was vulnerable and fragile now, he also was as immovable as the landmarks jutting up in the flat country. He'd come his distance; now she could come hers.

The poor man needed reassurance. He needed her care and she needed him to hold her, too—

Harmony threw up her hands. "I give up."

Moments later, she handed Jonah the picnic basket and muttered, "How like you." She tried not to look at him; he was too breathtaking. "If you only knew how much trouble it is to keep vegetable lasagna hot in the same basket with chilled wine. The salad won't be fresh at all...."

Jonah placed the basket in the buggy, placed his hat on top of it and drew her into his arms. "Hello, rosebud," he whispered huskily before his lips met hers.

His new mustache prickled and sensitized; she fitted her mouth to him once, twice, testing the texture. Then with delight, Harmony opened her lips to him.

When she recovered from his kiss, she was seated in the buggy, close to Jonah. He held the reins with one hand and her against him with his other. His exciting little kisses to her forehead, ear, nose and lips did nothing to soothe the humming warmth he had aroused with that first mind-blanking kiss.

"I had planned to be in charge of the evening...." Harmony managed between kisses and cuddling. She flattened her palms to the padded leather seat and the sensation of love warmed her skin. Other men had taken other women for moonlight rides and making up and loving.... Promises had been spoken beneath the buggy's fringed top and women had been treasured. A man had cried with joy when his beloved told him she carried his child. A teenage girl had decided that she was a woman and wanted to marry her young beau and she'd never regretted their young love.

Harmony nestled in the love feelings. She needed the comfort because Jonah certainly wasn't making her feel in control.

"That is some getup," Jonah stated admiringly, glancing at her.

"Well...yes. Just a basic black dress." Harmony smoothed the hem lower. Jonah's gaze was warming her moonlit knees. She knew he had her flustered, his typical effect on her. She knew she was losing control of the evening and the establishment of rules between them. Her need for Jonah overrode her schedules and all rules.

The horse clip-clopped softly, her heart raced and thudded and Jonah eased her head to rest on his shoulder. He nuzzled her hair and she wondered why everything was so right, but so confused, and why she couldn't make plans and keep to them, and—

"Do you still love me, rosebud?" Jonah asked softly.

She straightened away immediately, reminded of how she had bared her heart to him. Her infamous "I love you, you jerk" remark lingered in the night air.

"Well?" he prompted in that Western drawl. She sensed he was tense, afraid that his notions about this up-to-date city woman were old-fashioned.

While she loved his courtly ideas about moonlight rides, she had to keep a minimum of her pride.

"I'd rather not say," she stated primly. "I'm too put out with you right now."

"Dad courted Mother in this rig and Grandpa courted Grandma in it. It seemed right to take the woman who said she loved me riding in it."

Harmony's fingers locked to the arm of the wagon, sensing Jonah's other love. Whispers curled around the carriage—loving goodbyes.

"Yes," Harmony said simply as the wind curled around Jonah once, then was gone.

Love and tenderness layered the old polished leather seat and the fringed top swirled around Harmony. She smoothed the leather. "Where are we going?"

He smiled tenderly down at her as they crossed a field and began down into a coulee. "Worried about the lasagna, the wine or something else?"

"You . . . you have the ability to unnerve me, Jonah," she admitted softly, truthfully. "I had a plan for tonight. A step-by-step program."

"Were you unnerved when you said you loved me?" he asked too quietly as he pulled the reins and the buggy stopped in a cottonwood grove.

"Yes," she answered slowly, searching her heart. "You aren't what I had planned."

"Prespecifications?" he asked with a whimsical grin.

"Something like that."

The wind moved through the leaves, and the moonlight spread silver upon the lush grass. *This was a loving place... where Jonah had taken no one but her, and where he wanted to show her what lay within him.*

The night wind shook the leaves across the treetops and Harmony knew that long ago, other men and women had shared themselves here.

Jonah leapt from the buggy, a man of action to her contemplative mind. He raised his hands to her, and when her hand touched his, he reached to lift her into his arms.

"You're a loving woman, a caring, warmhearted woman," Jonah said slowly as he lowered her to stand in the lush grass.

Harmony discovered then that she had rushed to meet him so quickly that she had forgotten her shoes. "You unnerve me, Jonah," she repeated and wiggled her toes in the grass.

"Stay put," he said with a grin. Then he was carrying the basket and blanket toward cottonwood trees.

When he returned to her—a tall, lean masculine silhouette stroked by moonlight—she knew that Jonah would always return for what he wanted. A sense of ceremony and commitment eased her taut nerves, making her feel very certain and suddenly very—

"Shy?" Jonah asked softly, picking her up in his arms.

Harmony locked her arms around his neck and held him tight, shielding her blush in the warmth of his throat. "Frightened," she admitted truthfully.

"I'll keep you safe, rosebud," he whispered huskily.

Safe. She'd never been safe until Jonah held her like this, she decided.

When he eased to the blanket, and settled her on his lap, Harmony sat very still.

He leaned against a tree, gently pulled her closer to him and held her hands. His fingers were trembling around hers and she gathered their hands close to her heart.

"I've decided to start working the ranch again...to get back into wheat," he said thoughtfully. "It won't be easy. Long hours. To get started, I'll have to mortgage Fargo land. Anything could go wrong and crops could fail. I could lose the homestead."

"You won't."

He shifted her slightly and looked down at her tenderly. "How do you know so much?"

"Just a lucky, intuitive hit. And I know that you'll work for what you want . . . fight for it."

His smile was gentle. "Is that all?"

"I know you." She knew him very well, better than he perhaps knew himself. Because Jonah Fargo was the other half of her heart.

"You love me," he pushed teasingly and brushed a kiss across her lips.

Harmony trembled, reacting to her emotions instantly. "Well . . . yes. But it isn't easy."

"I'm an ornery old cuss," Jonah murmured agreeably, kissing her lashes and her nose.

"Yes, you are. And mean at times. You're closed-minded about things you can't see or smell or touch. You're irrational and moody and you act too quickly. And those are your good points." Since her ship was sinking, her methodical plans for the evening scuttled, she held him tight.

He nuzzled her cheek, filling her senses with his textures, his scents, his warmth. "I'd like to be quick right now, but I know you prefer the now-we-do-this, now-we-do-that method."

"Do I?" she asked, running her fingertips lightly over his mustache. "Schedules can be changed."

Ten

"**B**uckaroo, you are fast," Harmony declared unsteadily as Jonah settled over her. She arched into the hard thrust of his body and he gathered her closer, his body trembling—or was it hers? "I didn't know a cowboy could take off his boots that quickly."

In the space of two heartbeats, Jonah had eased her to her back, removed his boots and settled over her. She lay beneath him, breathing hard with her emotion, with what was to come....

Moonbeams slid through the cottonwoods, laying silver on Jonah's black hair as he braced over her, studying her. The grass crushed beneath the quilt released a fresh new scent of lives beginning and a new time. Harmony savored the taste, enveloping herself in the fragrance and nuances of this loving season.

Jonah ran his fingers through her hair, arranging it over the old quilt, spreading it out to the moonlight as if preparing for a ceremony that he would remember throughout his lifetime. "There is no one but you," he said slowly, huskily. "Sometimes I wonder if I didn't love enough...."

Dimmed memories of another love tugged at him briefly as she smoothed his forehead, running her fingertips across his eyebrows and across his closed lashes. "You loved enough, Jonah."

"This is different." Jonah slowly lowered his lips to hers, kissing her with tiny, testing, tantalizing bits of heat and desire as his hands reached beneath her to cradle her hips, lifting her to him. "You're a part of me, rosebud," he said unevenly against her throat.

"Jonah, you've got way too many clothes on," she whispered unsteadily, loving him, eager for them to be one.

Harmony's detached, in-control, calm, inner-self groaned. *There goes the evening schedule, shot to pieces. I knew I couldn't trust you next to this cowboy. You completely disregard your warning system whenever you're around him. You've got him staked out ready for... whatever!*

Harmony closed her eyes and inhaled. *I'm busy here. Do you mind?*

The reason for her self-control debate rolled to his back and lay looking at the starlit night, his hands folded behind his head. He looked delicious with delectable as a bonus.

Harmony lay stiffly at his side, her body longing for his and wondering what new twist Jonah had decided upon.

Jonah sighed leisurely as though he had all the time in the world. "I've never had a woman undress me before. It's been my fantasy," he said whimsically.

Harmony lay very still, considering her options. Jonah was unpredictable, too unreliable. She'd just lie here and maybe sleep a bit, because she wasn't jumping to his tune. She ordered her tensely poised, humming, Jonah-need to relax. She tried a quick dart into his thinking and found he was successfully blocking her. Left to his own devices, Jonah might revert to... to sleeping. He hadn't been getting enough lately.

No longer contemplating her schedule, Harmony-action-empowered woman quickly rose to her knees. She disregarded the tearing of her straps as she tugged off her dress, and placed her hand on his flat stomach. If he needed a claiming, another determined effort on her part, she'd give him one.

Jonah took her wrist and tugged her over him. "Are you coming for me, Miss Harmony?" he asked unsteadily against her lips as he slid away her bra.

"You bet I am. And you're not getting away," she returned, welcoming the warm pressure of his hands easing over her breasts. She closed her eyes, drawing in the pleasure of his callused palms cherishing her. When Jonah kissed a trail to her breasts, tasting first one then the other, Harmony caught his head and held him to her, her body quaking, warming, softening for his.

"You love me. . . . I can't believe it's true," he noted shakily, as she caught his hips with her thighs and gripped him tightly. When her hand found and caressed him, he tensed, brushing his lips against hers, tasting her lips with his tongue. "There's just you and me, rosebud, and love," he whispered, trailing very warm kisses to her ear. "Can you smell it? Like new grass growing and shedding the old. Like meadowlarks welcoming the sun and spring rain dripping from a flower into a pond."

She sniffed the scents, reveled in them around her, and attempted a Western endearment. "Sweeter than a honeybee on a field of clover?"

He smiled slowly and stretched leisurely beneath her as though snuggling beneath a comfortable downy quilt. "You're good."

"True," she returned breathlessly, concentrating on the mysteries of men's Western belts and jeans. She dismissed Harmony-in-control's warning to return to The Schedule. "Jonah, I can't undo your belt—" she exclaimed desperately as he skimmed away her briefs.

Jonah moved very fast for a big man, she thought in the next second, when he stretched out over her again without his clothes. "Hello, rosebud," he whispered gently as he found her intimately with his stroking fingers.

Someday we're going to do this nice and slow. Jonah's determined promise gave way to a hungry, longing groan.

Fine. Just fine. Lack of control all the way around. At least one of us has enough sense to keep calm. Your receptive reading talents never were in gear when your emotions take charge, you know. You could manage this whole thing better if you'd just not rush— Harmony's controlled self muttered as a sensual, tight ping shot through her. *Oh, shoot... there goes that one....*

She began to shiver, her heart trembling within her breast, her body aching to be his.

"Oh, rosebud," Jonah whispered longingly as if he were waiting for a homecoming he must have to survive.

When he slowly, luxuriously filled her, Harmony gripped him fiercely. "This is where you belong...this is where you belong," she repeated urgently, holding him so close that their bodies were one, that nothing lay between them.

"Yes..." Then Jonah smoothed her hips, lifting her higher and filling her so tightly in a way she'd never known before. They were so locked, so loving, as if they had always been part of each other.

Harmony began to shake, her body tightening, and she kept him closer, closer. Her teeth caught his shoulder, delicately tasting his skin, as they moved closer to the fire.

"We're in the flame," Jonah said against her skin, breathing heavily.

"Yes..." Harmony wrapped her arms and legs around him because he was hers and she was his and their hearts were racing home.

Jonah trembled wildly, running their race, and she fought for control and lost it, casting her fears into the night as their hearts beat, bodies and flesh melded by heat, by the urgent need that soared and burst and—

The horse nickered wildly, stomping in the field, and Harmony heard the high-pitched cry soar up into the night as Jonah held her close, his body poised very still, thudding deeply, intimately in hers.

Harmony looked up at him, her fingers locked to his tense shoulders, reluctant to free him to let him move into his separateness, away from her. "You're mine," she whispered as Jonah breathed heavily, his arms trembling with the effort of holding his weight.

He laughed then, looking glorious and delighted and very cocky. "You bet I am," he said, looking down at her with love.

Love lay on him, shining in his hair, in his eyes, in the curve of his lips touched by moonlight. It was just a matter of time before he knew it himself. Meanwhile, she would love enough for both of them.

She stroked his tense shoulders and slanted a wicked look at him. She'd never been this sensuous in her lifetime and Jonah was proving he could withstand her strength. She longed to pit herself against him, to enter the flames again. "I suppose we can eat now."

"Come here, you," Jonah said with a wide grin, as he eased down and rolled her over him.

"This is very..." she began, unsettled with the idea of straddling him in the moonlight.

"Intimate?" he asked as he arranged her trembling thighs closer and caressed the soles of her feet.

"Very." She gasped as he nuzzled her breasts, the caress leisurely when her tempo needs ran to overdrive. Harmony closed her eyes, reveling in his tasting, tempting exploration of her... now the inside of her elbow, now the tips of her fingers, the sensitive outer curve of her breast and slowly, too slowly down to circle her navel.

He was tracing her, exploring her, running his thumbs across her hipbones, then lower to her soft, sensitive femininity.... Tiny electric currents began rippling through her, her body tightening to hold him closer.

Harmony realized her fingers were rummaging through the hair on his chest, learning his textures, testing the beat of his heart beneath her palm. Jonah was her eternity; she'd circled her life, seeking and cold, and now with him she was whole....

"I like looking at you," he whispered, the deep sensuous tone curling around her like a caress. Then his finger eased under her necklace and he drew her down to him.

"Oh, Jonah," she returned unevenly, meeting his kiss with her hunger.

"We fit together," he said. "More than this, deeper than this, longer than this...." Then the heat wave hit them too quickly, shattering her leisurely enjoyment of the moment.

"Jonah?" she cried out, stunned by the pleasure rippling through her, holding her poised and breathless as sunlight burst into midnight stars and her pulse sang for his, blended with him.

Jonah curled his fingers into her hair and caught her close, his free hand caressing, anchoring, keeping her with him as she fought leaping into the fire, wanting to treasure the moment longer, clinging to the pleasure, keeping . . .

Then he turned her beneath him and she fought him, bringing him closer and then away, running from his pursuit, capturing his mouth with hers, riding the passion waves as each crest rose and broke and began again. . . .

"Harmony. . ." Jonah captured her hands, slid his fingers through hers and they gripped each other as the heat parted and they slid through, bursting, filling, keeping each other close as the flames burned, enclosing them.

Heartbeats later, Jonah breathed unevenly against Harmony's throat, his hand caressing her breast. He kissed the cupid riding her chest and his lips curved against her throat as she shivered. "Embarrassed?"

Harmony dug her fingertips into his back—his skin rippled delightfully beneath her touch. "No," she said too quickly and too righteously.

Jonah nuzzled her breasts and kissed the cupid pendant. "Mmm. Tiger woman captures man. Purrs while making love to man, then defeats man. Man is happy. Good to hear woman purr beneath him. Man want more, but man too tired."

She lay very still, the textures of Jonah new upon her, this new playful Jonah stunning her. "Are you teasing me, Jonah?" she asked carefully.

He chuckled and eased to her side, his fingers toying with her hair. "I've been roasted," he said in a cheery tone.

Harmony tensed, remembering now that she had held him with her heart and soul and body just as tightly as she could. She'd frightened him, taken more than he'd wanted to give—Her mind stopped rolling over problem rocks because her lanky cowboy mood changer was very busy. "Jonah, stop blowing in my ear. This is a serious moment."

"Oh, right. Serious," he agreed, then placed her hand on his chest, looked at the stars and began to sing "Home on the Range." When Harmony glared at him, he shifted into a James Brown Motown version of "I Feel Good."

She didn't feel too badly herself if her smile could be measured—she felt powerful, yet light, happy and aching and filled with wonder, somewhat like a child presented with a Christmas present she wanted very much. A happy, teasing cowboy doing an awful James Brown impersonation by moonlight was quite a present. Harmony sat up, curled her legs beneath her and lightly tugged his chest hair. His "ouch" was satisfactory and she smoothed the slight injury. Because uncertainty had touched her, she needed to sweep away the remains.

Jonah's hand smoothed her shoulders, staying her hand when she would have shielded herself with her dress. She held it up in the moonlight to study it. "I tore my dress," she exclaimed.

"Yes?" he prodded in an encouraging drawl and a wicked grin.

"Well. I certainly was . . . was engrossed at the time."

"You were mine and you knew it. Just like I knew part of me had finally come home. There is more to come, rosebud," Jonah said tenderly.

An image soared by her of Jonah's future lovemaking plans and she gasped. "Jonah, you kiss me there and I will not be held responsible for your safety."

But he was arranging her hair over her shoulders, smoothing the curls with his fingertips until his dark hand covered her pale breast. "Now tell me how you've never made love like this before, like you were being burned in the flames . . . like we were fused together too closely and so much a part of each other that nothing could tear us apart. Tell me that you've never made love so tight and fierce and way to the top, like you do with me . . . because it's true, isn't it? You've been afraid to let go—"

She cleared her throat, shielding her blush with her hair as she looked away. She remembered her dream when they first met, of this exact scene, the tender, loving, teasing Jonah, the flames fiercely joining them. "Well . . . true. This has been a unique experience. I mean I had a schedule for tonight, Jonah. You wrecked that immediately."

How many times had she whispered she loved him in that hot, fierce, wild flame?

"Are you sorry?" he asked gently, stroking her back.

"No," she returned fiercely. "You're what I want."

He lay there in the moonlight, staring at her as though he could look until his life eased through the years. Then she knew it was new for him, too, the fierce flames keeping them locked in heart and body, the gentle understanding later. Lifting her hair, Harmony unclasped her necklace and placed it around his throat.

Their eyes met. Each knew that more would come, their relationship would grow and bloom and— Harmony frowned slightly as Jonah's expression changed, shifted and an image slid by her. She blinked just once, the heat pouring from him, his needs driving again, wanting her. Her passion soared instantly, fueled by the currents running between them, images of dark and light skin moving in flames. His desire for her took away her breath, but it was no less than her own.

Then Jonah pulled her to him, their kiss hungry and urgent as they began again.

Jonah stirred restlessly at Harmony's side, her bed settling around them like a nest, easing them closer together in sleep. He dozed, cuddling her closer, sweeping his hands over her body, reclaiming her to him as he had done many times in the past two days. Harmony arched against his touch, snuggling against him as she sighed, and Jonah knew he was home. All that remained would settle into place....

When he awoke next, he was in a cold sweat, his body shaking. Or was he still wrapped by the tentacles of the nightmare?

"Jonah?" Harmony was shaking him, holding him fiercely, smoothing his hair from his damp forehead. "Jonah, wake up."

The child was crying... the dish containing rose potpourri near Harmony's bed slid off the nightstand; the tulip-shaped lamp was rattling— Jonah was running. Running toward the corridor. He was frightened... the blizzard was too fierce to leave Grace alone— "Grace?" he cried out, awaking fully. "Are you crying?"

Harmony's worried amber eyes peered over him and he realized that he was holding her wrist too tightly—she'd have bruises—and then he read the fear in her eyes.

He surged out of the bed they had shared—they had shared the entire house, making love slowly, tenderly or in a wild melody of happiness that they were together—

Harmony sat up in the froth of sheets, their clothing, and the bells on her wrist tinkled warningly. He jerked on his jeans and sat with his back to her to tug on his boots. "I'm leaving."

He had to run, to take his pain away from her.

Her fingers soothed his shoulders, her breasts nestled against his back as her arms came around him. "Jonah, don't move. We haven't . . . we haven't had time to talk about—"

"Leave it." He moved from her, afraid that what was in him would terrify her, would hurt her. It was better this way. Was he crying?

She was at the door before him, looking magnificent in a wild swirl of hair, her head held high as she pitted herself against him. She flattened her back to the door and shook her head.

He had to take his pain away—

"Jonah, you are not going anywhere," Harmony stated firmly, gathering her ruffled cotton robe around her—one that he had often stripped away from her, so hungry for their joining, so hungry for her warmth and the peace he knew with her.

"You don't know what's in my mind," he said slowly. "Now isn't the time." He wanted to gather her to him, to bury his face in that wild magnificent mane and tell her . . .

"Tell me, Jonah," Harmony stated too quietly.

He stared at her, his body rigid, trembling, sweating, barely leashed by his need to protect her. "No. Move away from the door, Harmony. I'm not certain now what's happening to me, but—"

She moved into him, against him before he could take a step. Harmony placed her hands on his damp cheeks, smoothing the beard she had enjoyed against her. Something sweet and warm quivered inside Jonah, remembering how she had loved him— how she had whispered of her love. "Hold me, Jonah," she asked, laying her body against his, into his care.

That gentle movement, her coming home, stopped him. "Harmony, now isn't the time . . ." he began, already gathering her to him.

She held him fiercely. He'd never been so close to anyone before. "Tell me, Jonah," she repeated. "Tell me what you know."

Then he was picking her up, holding her to him. He shook, too terrified that he would hurt her, too needy to let her go. "Before things happen, I see them. Not really, just impressions. I don't want this to happen to me...no more...no more...."

He told her what he'd never told anyone, this woman who loved him so fiercely, who kept near him so he could sleep, caring for him...who became his other part when they made love and in the past moments, a woman who knew him better than anyone ever had.

"I love you, Jonah. Remember that, darling...." Harmony was saying.

He closed his eyes, keeping her love wrapped in him, knowing it. When the trembling stopped, he eased into a chair and held her on his lap. With his face warmed by her scent, her wild silky hair, Jonah began to open his heart, his locked memories. "When I was a boy, I saw my father fall from that ladder...it seemed like a daydream then...then it happened and he died.... Other things happened. My wife—Maggie—I knew she shouldn't try to have another baby, not when we'd lost others...but she was so happy...so...."

He breathed deeply. "Then Grace...I'd seen her so cold...and then the wreck. I shouldn't have left her."

"Jonah, you had no choice. I've seen that ravine, that coulee. No one would have seen you."

"Maybe..." But he was reaching into the past, delving into other times. "I saw a three-year-old boy fall into the river.... I was already moving toward him when he actually did enter the water."

He looked at Harmony, not shielding his pain, his agony. "I'm losing my mind. Just when I've found you."

"You're not losing me, Jonah." Harmony stroked his tense, damp shoulders, smoothed his hair back from his forehead. "We've just found each other."

He shook his head. "I don't want you to be hurt by me. By what I might do—" He brought her wrist to his lips, kissing the sensitive skin that would wear his bruises in the morning.

Harmony drew his head to her, rocking him. "You are not leaving me, Jonah Fargo."

He closed his eyes, allowing her comfort to seep into him and clinging to the hope that she still loved him. How could she when this abyss quivered and hovered inside him?

Then Harmony was kissing him, taking him away from the terror.

He couldn't let her be hurt, Jonah thought, easing away gently from her. "No."

When he stood, chilled deeply without her, Harmony stood very still, fury lashing from her. "I am trying to understand, dear," she said too patiently. "I believe we shared something quite precious here in the last two days. Though you aren't what I wanted in my life, it seems I have no choice—because I love you. I believe we are bonded sufficiently."

"It's done," he said, his head aching... more memories, things he'd known would happen... they did happen... He'd keep Harmony from harm.

Harmony swept from the room and frightened for her, Jonah hurried to the bedroom, then her workshop. "It's for your good," he said to the shadows, her white cotton robe catching the moonlight like fear in the night.

"Really? Listen carefully, Jonah. I am not removed so easily from your hard times. When we met—when you were determined to have mind-blanking sex with June Fields—I saw you and a woman inside a flame, burning, bonding forever with your bodies, your hearts...." Harmony took a deep breath and whirled away, her hand gripping Therapy's horn, her eyes glistening damply. "And that, Jonah, is what I saw... what you saw when I gave you my necklace... and why you will *not—repeat—not* leave me now. Until we are finished. Until the proverbial last note of the overweight lady's song is finished. Because Jonah, I am that woman and nothing matters but you and me—together."

She shimmered in the dim light, her hair catching reddish tints. Jonah realized she was fighting now, struggling to hold him with her and yet fearing he'd moved away. He touched the cupid pendant nestled on his chest, remembering how she had given herself to him and the flames that had caught them, igniting them.

He'd seen those images, the man and the woman bonding in the flames, and he saw Harmony now, fighting for their love. "I can't understand what is happening to me, Harmony. I don't want it."

"You have it. Jonah, you are a seer. Those images you saw before the events—"

"You're not giving an inch, are you?" he asked roughly, trying to find reason in the way they shared images of the man and the woman bonding in the flames. He'd seen the woman place her necklace on him, claiming him for her own.

You are not leaving me now. Not like this, a feminine voice declared firmly, and Jonah sensed the pain running through Harmony, her uncertainties, her love for him. He needed her again, to have the other part of his soul and heart joined to him, making him whole....

Their eyes locked across the distance of the workshop and Jonah felt Harmony tremble. "You may go now," she stated suddenly, her fierce pride sweeping through her as she gripped the metal monster.

"It's pretty hard to move when you're holding that horn, rosebud," he said unevenly, wanting desperately to hold her, to cherish her.

"Well, then, buckaroo, you'll just have to come and get me, because I am not letting go."

He walked slowly toward her and without releasing her gaze, he took her hand from Therapy and lifted it to his lips. "Hold on, rosebud," he whispered, stepping into the scents and warmth of her. "But you don't need this any longer," he said as he unfastened her bracelet and placed it over Therapy's horn.

"Jonah, you don't know. Without my alarm system, I could be dangerous, open to any sort of impulses. You might not be safe."

"Uh-huh. Sounds good," he whispered, lowering his lips to hers as he lifted her into his arms.

Two weeks later, July spread over the dry, ageless Montana land. Jonah worked every waking hour, trying to reclaim Fargo land for wheat farming.

While Harmony didn't like him leaving, she understood that he needed to work out his fears, to control and seek what was in him. Had his Blackfoot grandmother given him a psychic heritage?

According to the psychic books that Harmony had boxed and plopped on his doorstep, whatever was humming in him could be recognized as psychic abilities.

The hard physical work was good, cleansing him, but the nights too long without Harmony. When he was whole—understanding what had or could happen to him—he'd claim her. Jonah didn't want to be a man needing her strength, a lover too weak to care for her.

"Pride," she had stated flatly when he told her he was leaving, but that she was a part of him. "Pride and arrogance. You are in for real trouble now," she had muttered against his shoulder where she had been crying.

I love you, he had thought, wedging the thought firmly in his mind. *You are in my heart.*

"Oh, sure. In your heart," she had repeated, holding him closer.

I have to work this out.

Work it out here, with me.

"Harmony?" he had asked shakily. "What is happening between us?"

Figure it out, she thought grumpily.

I'll be coming for you—

You can't expect me to... Oh, sure. Ugh. You woman, me man. That cowboy logic went out at the turn of the century. Let me help you, Jonah...

No.

Her dark gold eyes, dimmed by tears had flashed up at him, his tiger woman. *We are not pleased,* she thought royally, then blinked when he rubbed her nose with his.

"Ohh!" she exclaimed in a frustrated tone; then she threw her arms around him for a kiss to last until their time came again.

He missed her like he missed a portion of his heart. He understood the bonding and the mating terms that had been circling him, humming through his life. Yet the crying hadn't stopped, and each time he stared at the doll, waiting for answers, he ached more.

Just a doll, the lacy material wrinkled and worn from his handling. A little baby doll ... He stroked the gown and whispered, "Shh, Grace. Go to sleep."

He sensed the cupids guarded him as he searched the shadows. The warmth of Harmony's love surrounded him, her metal monsters gleaming in the sun.

Harmony's royal "we" weren't happy lately. In the two weeks since they'd made love—when June slid into July—she'd fretted about him and he'd ached for her. Very little kept him from bringing her to Fargo land. But he would not wake up in terror beside her, bruising her fragile, pale skin while he dealt with his shifting mind.

The *Fascinating Homes* lady reporter was determined that he was hiding a fabulous decor in his home and had crawled through his open window one day. Jonah sensed her disappointment and received an "I am aghast, simply aghast" reading from her. Lucky was busy with June and Shrimp had deserted him completely, though she was glad to see him when he dropped by Shep's statue. Lately, one of the farmers had parked his pickup near her post and a handsome male collie had been eyeing her....

The land had waited. He'd felt it rise up to greet and to challenge him that first morning; he'd settle his life, work through his problems and then he'd claim Harmony, his other half.

The middle of July heat soaked into Fort Benton's historical brick buildings and spilled onto the shaded street.

Jonah, dirty and sweaty, drove into town for a tractor part. He parked his pickup beside Harmony's on the street. She emerged from a store, dressed in her workclothes and boots, and promptly leveled a glare at him. *So. Happy are we?*

I'm making progress. That spy you sent, the Fascinating Homes *lady crawled through my bedroom window.*

Humph. With my cupids, you have plenty of company. Harmony tossed her head and swept by him to open her truck door. *Out of my way, Fargo—you hardheaded, swaggering, grinning, wicked—*

Mmm. I love it when you talk like that, little sweetheart.

She stood between their trucks with him, so close, he could smell her skin, see those wide amber eyes open to his soul.

"How are you, Jonah?" she whispered, running her fingers lightly over his cheekbones, his tense jaw and across his lips.

"Missing you. Wanting you," he returned, turning to place a kiss in her palm.

She closed her fingers over the kiss and brought it to her heart. "Keep safe, love," she said achingly.

"Harmony?" He had to know...

"Yes?"

"Are we talking aloud or in our minds?"

I love you, Jonah. Keep safe, she repeated without moving her lips.

The next day, Jonah—again dirty and sweaty—was talking to Lucky about new machinery when Harmony emerged from a store and began to walk toward them, her hair standing out wildly, catching the sunlight in reddish sparks.

I'd like to make love to you right now, Jonah thought, focusing his thoughts on Harmony.

No way. You're working things out. Remember? she shot back, her amber eyes lighting furiously as she came closer. *Don't try those little happy caresser feelers on me, Jonah. I'm not in the mood.*

I'd do a lot more than that if I weren't so dirty.

To test his thoughts—or were they hers?—Jonah concentrated on Harmony's breasts, shielded beneath her loose-flowing shirt. He thought of the rosebud tips, the soft pale round—

You will not touch me, Jonah Fargo. I can't be available for your every little feeler whimsy, just when you are in the mood. You know very well that you could be exploring your powers while we are in the same vicinity. All this...self-imposed study without me is really steaming me. We are not pleased, she thought, using the royal "we."

I'm working on my program, rosebud. I have a real problem concentrating on mind matters when you're around.

You're working on your pride. I don't think I like you very much right now. Get lost, you jerk. There's two of us in this relationship. Or supposed to be. When you figure that out, we'll chat.

He focused on her sweetness, on the heat that had welcomed him, and Harmony's lips parted in a gasp as she closed her eyes and stood still, her face flushing to his delight.

Then her amber eyes flashed open. *You big buckaroo! Lay off.*

Make me. Because he was happy and in love, Jonah tilted back his hat, hooked his thumbs in his belt and stood grinning at her.

You want to play rough, do you? Harmony frowned and studied him, from hat to boots, and Jonah shivered, as in his mind, her hands were exploring him, finding the cupid buried beneath his shirt, then sweeping lower.

His chest tightened as her mouth heated it, her teeth nibbling on him tantalizingly. *Rough? Do 'we' call that rough?* he thought, inhaling sharply as Harmony walked closer.

She stopped between their trucks and looked up at him. *I told you that without my bracelet I will not be held responsible. Get out of my way.*

You're an exciting tiger woman when you're riled, Miss Harmony.

She flicked him a glance. *Trust me, cowboy. You really don't want to try my powers now. You'd better get yourself to someplace safe and take that gorgeous mustache with you.*

Anytime you're ready, Jonah thought with a wide grin, and wiggled his mustache as he imaged her soft stomach.

She inhaled and placed her hand over her stomach, pressing her loose shirt and jeans tightly against her.

You asked for this. Harmony's dark gold eyes became enormous in her lightly tanned face. Her body warmed his, that soft womanly scent swirling up and around him in the bright July sunlight. Jonah swallowed tightly as he saw her body ease into his, stir her breasts against him and settle over him intimately.

He locked his boots to the street and held his breath as Harmony made hot, quick love to him. Jonah leaned against the pickup for support and pictured his body clenching, his hands, his mouth filling with Harmony's sweetness.

We're standing here between two pickups in broad daylight. You are not making love to me now, rosebud. If you are, I'm too dirty....

Aren't I? This is for your own good, Jonah. Well, maybe mine, too. Don't count on farm dirt to keep you safe from me. So hold on to something real and do it fast, because I can't stop now.

His image of Harmony moved strongly over him, on him, taking, giving, wanting, needing.

In his mouth, her skin tasted like rose petals, her pulse meeting his as their passion grew and burst.

Jonah gripped his pickup's door handle as he saw colors, his mind and body arching into Harmony's, giving himself to her, taking...

Jonah sagged against the pickup, drained.

Then she was kissing him, bringing his head to her breasts, comforting him. Or was she?

When he summoned the strength to blink, Harmony was fully dressed, straightening her hair and trembling. "So that's how it is, buckaroo," she murmured briskly, getting into her pickup. "Get used to it. You wanted me not to wear my bracelet and you deserved every—"

"I sure did, rosebud," Jonah managed to say as he leaned heavily against the pickup. "You just keep that bracelet off when you're around me, because the next time you pull a stunt like this, I'll be ready."

Her eyebrows lifted disbelievingly. "Really? Remember, buckaroo, I've had time to adjust to my powers. This is a dimension where big muscles and cocky grins don't cut it."

"I'll get the hang of it," he promised darkly, resenting his weakness now.

"Anytime, buckaroo," she challenged, reversing the pickup to pull away. "By the way, I love you."

Jonah gripped his door handle and hoped his legs wouldn't collapse. Shrimp sent him a knowing grin and Lucky appeared on the sidewalk.

"Hot, isn't it?" Lucky asked conversationally, around the toothpick in his mouth. He looked at Jonah. "Man. Don't you look gooney. Real lathered up and sort of weak. Is the heat getting to you, sweetheart?"

Eleven

"**S**tubborn cowboy. An unfit host for my sweet little cupids," Harmony muttered darkly. She skidded the pickup to a stop and ran inside her house.

Without Jonah, her warm, comfortable home seemed empty. "He deserved that for testing me right there on the street. For taking my bracelet off. It's open season on him now. I didn't want him, but I love him and that's how it is. Trust me to fall in love with an unpredictable man, whose pride won't let me help him through his dark times."

Harmony hugged herself and stared out into the golden wheat fields baking in the July sunset.

Jonah had looked tired, dirty and sweaty, his work clothes tattered and grimy with oil. His unshaven cheeks were hollow, the shadows under his eyes told an aching tale.

Her fingers bit into her upper arms as she realized how proud this man was, how he wanted to protect her and understand himself. She had to give him time . . . but that did not make the waiting easier.

The last day of July, Harmony stormed into the post office for her mail. She'd spent too many aching, sleepless hours waiting for Jonah.

Very little kept her from vamping him . . . from riding to his ranch and loving him.

The *Fascinating Homes* reporter had insinuated that she and Jonah were *very* good friends; according to the "city blonde," Jonah would be letting the reporter decorate his home soon.

Jealousy wasn't a hair bow that Harmony wore well. Who did Jonah think he was anyway? Here she was, already done sorting through her Mark inhibitions, and waiting for Jonah to make his appearance.

She crushed the envelopes in her mailbox as she began to draw them out, while thinking about how she would make Jonah pay for his too-long interlude. She refused to be reasonable on this point.

After all, he'd removed her bracelet alarm and he was liable to suffer the consequences.

Oh, sure, she loved him. But there were limits to her stability—her senses were humming on overdrive, wanting Jonah near her, wanting his reassurance and cuddling. . . . This time, a burned peach pie and an adorable kitten would not cut it.

Morning, rosebud. Jonah's low, sexy Montana drawl swirled around Harmony's mind.

Her fingers crushed her mail even more as she slowly closed her mailbox. Jonah's hard body moved against her back and his hands rose to cup her breasts intimately, his thumbs running tantalizingly over the tips.

Surprised as his desire settled intimately against her, his hard thighs thrusting against hers, Harmony stopped breathing. She nestled back against Jonah's desire and knew that he was tossing an image at her. An irresistible, delectable, body-responding hot, desiring image. She closed her eyes as a wave of pleasure surged over her, the Jonah image cupping her breasts and nuzzling the side of her throat, and pressing intimately against her backside. Passion was already racing through her, the need to make them one . . .

She glanced over her shoulder to find Jonah leaning against the wall, several feet away from her, watching her with slumberous, sensual dark blue eyes. She'd been too wrapped in her emotions to sense him near her. Her lips parted with a slight gasp as his image stepped closer and filled her. Jonah's lips against her throat and every one of his loving feelers stroked her from head to toe as she tightened every intimate muscle, welcoming him.

Harmony gripped her mail with one hand as waves of steamy, warm, quaking pleasure burst over her. Jonah's image was making love to her, gently, yet hungrily, and she closed her eyes, braced herself against the post office wall and took every wave of pleasure within her.

She trembled, pictured his image flushed and intense over her, holding her, their bodies straining, making love without clothing.

Breathing rapidly, Harmony realized that she had been holding her breath as Jonah caressed her, his mouth tantalizing her breasts, nibbling, cherishing.

She clung to him as he lifted her over his hips, joining them.

She was complete then, hot and bursting with each hungry kiss, fighting for the ultimate pleasure as Jonah carried them on.

Then he was soothing her, cradling her near him, murmuring sweet tender thoughts while she lay against him, melted into one warm, drowsy, happy heap.

Harmony swallowed, forced her head to lift and realized that she was flushed and damp and boneless, leaning against the post office wall.

Gathering every bit of her strength, she looked at Jonah who remained in his corner of the post office, apart from her, fully dressed in his cotton shirt, faded jeans and boots.

His lips pursed to blow her a kiss and then she knew.... "You've been practicing, buckaroo," she managed softly as she straightened away from the wall and smoothed her hair with trembling fingers. She gathered her mail to her aching breasts and walked unsteadily toward him.

He lifted her fingers to his lips and nibbled them. Then he placed her palm over his rapidly beating heart and she knew that he had also run his race with passion. "I miss you, rosebud," he said huskily, his hand trembling as he smoothed her hair and brought it to his lips.

"I'd prefer the real thing.... There could be psychics out there who are going to get the strangest readings from their mail," she whispered darkly as Mrs. Jones passed by, eyeing them. "Don't ever pull that on me again. You no longer have the protection of my bells, you know."

His fingertip smoothed her hot cheek. "Anytime. Seems fair to me."

"Nothing is fair. Not when it comes to you."

"Do you still love me?"

"You know I do. Why? I wonder. Don't ask me. You keep hoarding yourself over there, doing heaven only knows what, and I may just raid your fort. It's not cool to sort through your new psychic discoveries without the person who loves you."

"You're right and I'm a low-down skunk. Life's dull on the prairie without my little dew-drenched daisy," Jonah murmured sadly. His tone was at odds with the humor lighting his face.

"I'll show you dew-drenched daisy if you pull anything like this again," she threatened shakily, wanting his arms around her.

Come here, rosebud, Jonah mind-murmured, actually drawing her into his arms and cuddling her.

You are crushing my mail, she protested without malice, snuggling deep in his arms.

Jonah's hands stroked her back. *I need you here. I'm getting closer to understanding . . . it's difficult.*

Of course it is. It's painful to realize.

I don't want . . . powers.

I know, but you don't have to develop them. . . . They don't have to be the focus of your life. You'll learn how to control and when to step into them.

I want you. After harvest, I'll be coming for you. The choice is yours. I can't make any promises about . . . about—

She lifted her head, looking into his dark blue eyes. *I come with my powers. Yours are to do with as you wish— What kind of an invitation is 'I'll be coming for you'?*

His fingertip traced the contour of her lips. *You'll know what is right. But I want you. You're my heart, my life. . . . I want to come to you as a man, a complete man.*

Great. Fine. Whatever. Take care of yourself. Harmony clenched his shirt. *I love you, you big muley jerk.*

My, my. How you sweet-talk, he teased, his lips curving. Then he stilled and she listened to their hearts beating as one. *I'll come for you after harvest.*

"So he's coming for you? What does that mean? Marriage?" Pax sat in the kitchen, sipped his herbal tea and watched Harmony pack the dishes that had been handed down from their grandmothers. August had passed, a hot, lonely month without Jonah, and September's first week had arrived.

Harmony peered out the window for the thousandth time. Harvest was over. September lay in cool nights, and geese were heading south.... Pronghorn antelope blended into the golden fields, their white rumps bounding away when they were frightened.

She carefully wrapped tissue around the old china. She'd been packing for two weeks and still Jonah's pickup hadn't come. He'd been hauling lumber and carpenter supplies from town and had ordered wooden spokes for a wagon. He'd gone shopping for new jeans and shirts. Though June was too busy running from Lucky's pursuit, the *Fascinating Homes* lady had been circling Jonah.

Harmony ran her fingers over the old crystal that had been her great-great-grandmother's bridal gift.

"Pax, repairing an old, horse-drawn wagon might be something a man would do in the winter, when there wasn't any outside work, wouldn't it?"

She inhaled, holding the crystal to her. Her fears leapt at her. Jonah had changed his mind. He was afraid of her now—afraid of her irrational emotions when she was near him, her explosive temper, her Amazon strength and her blazing love of him, let alone her powers.

Jonah was living up to her picture of the unsuitable love mate.... She should have stuck to her prespecifications for an easygoing, rational man. "Pax, there are two people in this relationship and one of them is keeping to himself. Somehow that is not an equal sharing of hearts."

Today she'd dressed in a worn flannel shirt, jeans and her work boots. Since Jonah had not appeared, she had decided to dress in work clothes. The romantic blouses and skirts she'd been wearing, just for his arrival, slipped off her shoulders and got in the way of welding. They didn't match her leather apron, and she'd grown tired of lacing and unlacing her work boots to change into slippers. Her new lacy underwear showed wear from daily hand washings.

Pax looked at her. "He'll come. You look stormy," he said.

"I love that jerk. He's stubborn, ornery and absolutely unpredictable. If he waits much longer, I'm starting a mate for Therapy. I'll have a matching set."

Pax raised his hand in a warning gesture. "Now, don't get too revved up. The world isn't ready for another Therapy. If Jonah said he will come for you, he'll come. He's been working in the wheat harvest. He's mortgaged his land and is trying to get back on his feet. That takes money. A crop failure or hail could take away everything. He is a proud man. He's probably trying to repair his house. Men like to make their nests cozy for their ladyloves just the way women do."

Harmony sniffed disbelievingly. "That's old range-cowboy garbage. He knows he doesn't have to do that. I just want to be with him. According to my sources, he's fixing some old wagon. He's painting something red, probably his barn. Red won't go with my copper cupids. He's taking time to repair a team-harness rig while I'm wearing come-hither dresses and eating too much. Do you know how hard it is to work with metal and keep your lace from snagging? When I get him in my clutches, he'll—" She tilted her head. "Pax, do you hear something?"

He held aside the curtain to look out the window and Harmony came to stand beside him.

Two heavily built workhorses were pulling an old-fashioned wooden hauling wagon toward her house. Easily recognizable in his Western hat, Jonah sat in the driver's seat, holding the reins. A colorful array of balloons clung to the wagon and ribbon streamers circled it.

Harmony blinked, noting the way the horses manes and tails were groomed and decorated with big ribbons and bows. "Now? Now he's coming in that?"

Pax's roaring laughter followed her out the door. She ran toward Jonah, aware of only him and the happiness swirling in her.

He had stopped the wagon and was walking quickly toward her, carrying a big bouquet of wildflowers and wheat.

They met in a flurry of hungry kisses and promises. Jonah lifted and whirled her around him as they laughed, crushing the huge bouquet and kissing each other over it. He was still holding her off the ground when Pax walked toward them, carrying a packed box. "She's been wearing off-the-shoulder, frilly dresses every day until today. You're going to pay for making her wait, my friend," he said to Jonah who was grinning as Harmony placed another flurry of kisses across his face.

"Maybe she'll let me live. Look," Jonah said, turning her toward the wagon.

She grabbed his head and whispered urgently into his ear, "Jonah, don't image anything . . . anything too intimate. Pax can read."

Jonah slowly looked at Pax, who was grinning widely. "He'd better not be able to read long-distance, because I have big plans and they don't include him," Jonah muttered.

She laughed, happiness bubbling out of her into the September sunshine. "What did you want to show me?"

Jonah continued to hold her off the ground and to study Pax. "You, too?"

"All my life. I haven't used my powers until Harmony arrived and then just to tease her. They are weaker than my sister's. Somehow I've managed to keep a balanced life. A good life. My son is displaying ability now. Janice is terrified, but trying to understand."

Jonah inhaled unsteadily and Harmony held him close. "That was one of the reasons Pax wanted to move here, to work out his problems and help Janice understand. He felt they needed space from other people as their children developed. For some reason—we think she was terrified—our mother forced her powers away, and hated ours when they began to emerge. It was painful for us as children. Pax wants space and the friendliness of this community to raise his children."

She stroked the taut muscles in Jonah's neck, aching for him. His eyes were sky-blue bright as they pierced hers. "I've brought you Fargo wheat. It's the customary bridal gift, and that bouquet is all I've got to offer now. Our life will be good, I promise."

Harmony lovingly stroked the dry wheat stalks. "I know. I saw what you imaged while you were driving this wagon. You saw the men in your family going after their brides, claiming them forever. Is that how you see me, as your sweet little rosebud bride, fresher than cow's milk steaming in the bucket?"

Jonah blushed, his skin heating beneath her fingertips. "I just might have a disgusting romantic streak. It's too early to tell. It might be just another power," he admitted in a low disgusted grumble. "I should have left off the cow's milk remark, right? This *thinking* sweet talk isn't easy, you know. I was practicing and my concentration ricocheted straight into that city woman. I had to hide on the roof beside one of your cupids until she left."

"Poor little cowboy. I'll protect you from now on. I'll capture every little loving thought you have and hold it close to my heart. Show me what you wanted to earlier, love." Harmony knew she'd enjoy exploring Jonah's romantic nature. He'd proven to be very gallant, old-fashioned and cherishing. Add a dash of teasing, boyish play and James Brown's Motown, and the whole lanky cowboy package was pretty fascinating.

On the side of the wagon he had painted a big, red I Love You.

"It's a hard thing to say—those three words," Jonah stated in his wise, Western cowboy tone. "Must take practice. Lucky saw me practicing it. I didn't know he could run like that."

When she began to cry, curling against him, Jonah kissed her cheek and carried her to the other side of the wagon. There on the wooden boards was another red message. Will You Marry Me?

I love you, Harmony. Will you marry me? Jonah was asking silently, his eyes bright with emotion.

"Oh, yes," she answered. "Yes, yes, yes!"

Her fingers trembled, running over the smoothly shaven contours of his cheeks, his jaw, testing the mustache and trailing across his lips. He kissed her fingertips. *I accept what I am. What we are, my love.*

We are one, my heart.

Three weeks before Christmas, Jonah stopped on the street and let his senses open to the little girl and her unhappy mother.

The six-year-old girl, Mary, stood with her face pressed against the store window, wishing for her Christmas doll. Beside her, her mother wished she could give her daughter a special gift—they had so little. With the scraps and lace she'd been saving, she could sew dresses and a blanket for a doll. But Mary's beautiful doll would have to wait until a better time, another Christmas.

Jonah fought the familiar clenching of his heart, the ache that had gentled with his understanding that he had to let Grace go....

He'd mourned too long, cradling his pain and fighting his abilities. With Harmony's help, he understood that he could balance his life, and yet that he had inherited a special gift. A man who was loved and loved back didn't have much heart room for aching, doubts and loneliness.

He still awoke to the child crying, though not often now. There was an easing in him, love replacing the sadness, the bitter frustration and guilt. When the shadows came, gentle images of Harmony soothed him and he wrapped them around him.

Excitement raced through their marriage, his love and fascination for Harmony growing each day. He loved to tease her, to catch her close and reveal his heart. Their lives were busy, happy and sweet. Their loving times were tender, fiery and frequent. Harmony worked by his side, never doubting that he would keep Fargo land safe, that the first crop would be magnificent. She didn't need psychic powers to know that, she'd said with a toss of her head. She just knew her husband.

Later that night, Jonah carried Grace's doll to the girl's house. When he gave the doll to the woman, she began to cry quietly. She clutched his gift and managed a tearful thank-you.

Jonah sat in his pickup for several minutes after he arrived at the home he shared with his wife. He'd wondered how many more times Harmony would watch him focus on the child's crying? How much more of his unsettled past would she feel before leaving him?

But understanding and love swirled around him each time he doubted himself, each time he awoke to the nightmare or caught the sound in the wind.

He listened to the winter wind outside his pickup, listened to the echoes in the shadows of the snow-covered plains. The sounds were that of his heart opening, of the past's pain easing. He focused on the sounds, listening with the powers that he had accepted as a part of his life. The sweeping wind cleansed and nourished and the crying had stopped. "Goodbye, Grace," he murmured to the wind. "See you."

Jonah? Oh, you're here! How I've waited...how I love you, Harmony's tender thoughts leapt into his mind and he turned slowly to see her outlined in the doorway—his future, his love, his life.

Impulsive, emotional, she ran into the slicing wind. She ran to him, dressed in her boots, jeans and his shirt. Jonah smiled briefly as he hurried to her.

Across the Fargo rooftops, the copper cupids and weather vane wore twinkle lights and the cupid wind chimes created unlikely Christmas carols. He wasn't certain if he could tolerate the new Therapy she'd been working on while giving him space to make his decisions.

They met in a gust of snowflakes and Jonah scooped her up to his chest. Harmony's familiar scents enclosed him. He tucked his face in her hair and picked through her Christmas baking, her flowery intimate scents to the one that he knew well—his other half, his heart and soul. Filled with emotion, Harmony's mind swirled around him, over him, too busy to know he was treasuring each loving thought. Along the way, she was thinking that he was ornery—leaving her to worry about him. She just might not tell him about the peach pie she'd baked, or the cupid she'd welded to Therapy's tail while she was waiting. She never, never wanted to be parted from him again. What if something had happened to him?

I'm just fine, rosebud. Slow down. You're getting yourself worked up to explode.

You big, infuriating, low-down yahoo. Of course I'm upset. You just decide to do things...no warning at all. You just don't schedule one thing in our entire lives. I was worried about you. Do you know how hard it is to shop for a reasonable, companionable man? Then come up with someone as unpredictable as you are? Do you know how hard it is to find a heart mate, the other part of my life, my mind, my soul? I'm certain that there are enough frozen cavemen already without adding you to their number.

Sheltering her from the wind, he carried her back to the house while she continued to clutch and hug him, and mentally fuss over what areas of his anatomy were frostbitten. Jonah found himself smiling. He liked her fussing over him, scolding and threatening him with dire consequences if he. . . .

ever pull a trick like that again, I won't be held responsible. Even though your powers are developing, I'm still stronger in the imaging department. You won't get out of this with that rose-petal-raining-into-our-bed trick this time. If you ever leave me without warning to travel into a blizzard again, I swear I will personally place a cupid on every Fargo fence post. I'll enter you in love-god contests from here to every psychic possible.

"You'll catch cold, rosebud," he said aloud when she paused.

She gathered him to her and held him tightly. "Then I'll drink rosehip tea and snuggle close to you. You are a sweet, dear man, Jonah Fargo," she whispered fiercely, tears trailing down her cheeks as she kissed him. *You are free, aren't you, dear one?*

"It was time, rosebud. It was time," he repeated, needing to say the words aloud. His heart eased, a sadness flowing through him and away into the bitter, cutting wind. Harmony understood how he had ached, giving up that last precious tie to his daughter, though she would remain with him forever.

"I do love you," Harmony murmured against his cheek, shivering and burrowing closer to him.

"My heart, my life," Jonah whispered, holding her close after he'd shut the door with his boot.

"Likewise," she whispered against his lips. Then she splashed him with cupids and imaged reindeer horns with jingle bells on his head.

Jonah began to laugh and fell with her onto the couch. He shook his head, rattling the bells on his imaged reindeer horns. She looked up at him, love shining in her expression as she said, "Welcome home, cowboy."

Epilogue

————

Harmony shivered, blinked, smoothed her hair shakily and then her clothing, as she continued carrying Jonah's Santa Claus suit to him. *"That was not funny,"* she muttered aloud, gripping their bedroom dresser with a supporting hand.

She blew a tendril from her flushed face and frowned at him. "We are not amused. Making love to me while I'm acting as a hostess isn't fair play, buckaroo. You know Pax's entire family is waiting in the living room for Santa Claus. Now was no time to ambush me."

Jonah drew her into his arms and knew that she'd come for him in the night when the house was quiet, when she could revel in her powers as a loving wife and tiger woman. She pushed him back onto the old bed and pinned him beneath her, crushing Santa's pillow stomach and grinning at him over it. Jonah smoothed his way through her hostess lace and cranberry velvet dress to caress her thigh. She quivered at his touch, her amber eyes dark with sated passion and a touch of revenge.

"I couldn't wait," he admitted ruefully as he smiled, still woozy and happy from their lovemaking. "You look so caressable. My loving feelers went wild. They stampeded toward you in this Christmas getup. I can't be held responsible, especially when you pet that new monster's horn.''

''When I hold Therapy's horn, I'm working on my new designs or some deep, vast problem, like your nonscheduled behavior, and you know it. Just you wait. When I catch you under the mistletoe ball, you're going to melt, Mr. Fargo,'' she threatened with a wicked grin.

''Mmm. Promises, promises.'' Then he sighed happily and stretched beneath her.

Harmony kissed him leisurely, trimming off the passion still humming through them. ''If we didn't have a house filled with guests and children waiting for Mr. Ho Ho, I'd pay you back for your little ambush.''

''Little?'' He wrapped her hair around his fingers, studying the textures and scent of his wife, his love. He imaged Harmony later, after Pax's family had gone. His wife looked adorable in the Santa Claus hat and her black nightie.

''I refuse to patronize you. Lately you are far too confident.'' Her fingers smoothed the cupid pendant beneath his sweater and love filled her amber eyes. ''I do love you, buckaroo.''

Harmony sat on Jonah-Santa's lap and cuddled close to his pillow stomach. She smiled at Pax, Janice and the children who had gathered around Santa Claus. ''I've got everything I want, Santa,'' she said, meaning it.

She settled drowsily against him, laying her head on his Santa-clad shoulder. ''Everything,'' she repeated, filled with happiness as she looked at each loving face.

She surveyed the home that she and Jonah had begun to redo, the huge Christmas tree twinkling in the corner, the scents and delights of Christmas shared with her loved ones.

The months since Jonah's claiming were thrilling as she adjusted to her fast, unpredictable, but always desirous, sweet and old-fashioned, cowboy-husband.

Jonah had insisted on a proper church wedding with all the frills. He had insisted on a white dress and grimly refused to participate in any image-loving in the week before their mid-September wedding. As a pregroom, he meticulously outlined possible crop failures, his morning moods and how he was very happy without children in their lives. Pax's brood was too much anyway.

She sensed a bit of untruth in that statement, but their love grew every day. Now she found Jonah looking at her, because he seemed to like that activity, and the moment she locked onto his fast-moving thoughts, she caught images of herself in a Santa Claus cap and a black negligee.

Jonah was determined to understand himself and to make their marriage work. He did not promise to understand her, just to love her with every bit of his heart. He said that she was too emotional, too susceptible to womanly irrationalities, but despite all that, he flat-out loved her because "all of her rosebud components went together just fine."

He studiously said "I love you" every morning and every night and meant it. After their marriage, he mused frequently and Harmony had wondered, too, if they could damage body parts by constant lovemaking, psychic or real. They shared the quiet times, the gentle silent understanding times, and she listened with Jonah to the sweeping sigh of the wind.

Since he'd given away the doll, Jonah's pain had eased. He missed his daughter, but his heart had gentled, filled with Harmony's love and their future.

Jonah was considerate, teasing, boyish and all-Western male. When faced with choices such as linoleum colors or curtains, he reverted to spouting safe, ancient cowboy wisdom.

Harmony had learned how to ride horses, how to sing to distraught cows during thunderstorms and how to tell when the diggings were good for "bones"—dinosaurs'. She learned how to whistle without using her fingers, to call a horse. Jonah was very proud of her farm-machinery-welding skills and her cautious ability to ease troubled friends.

He'd forgiven her when she was really angry and dressed him in a suit of bells. Harmony yawned and cuddled closer to Jonah-Santa. Jonah had stood, grinning and challenging her, and she'd thrown the bells at him.

Now, on their first Christmas Eve as Mr. and Mrs. Fargo, Harmony nestled in Jonah-Santa's strong arms and sighed sleepily.... She'd been moving very fast, her life in constant tilt since their marriage. There was the open house and Jonah acting proudly as she showed off her new shop, a modernized block building. Neighbors came frequently and she and Jonah had quite the social life, in and out of Fort Benton socials. Lucky brought June to Thanksgiving dinner. A proud cowboy, Lucky treated the blushing and sometimes-flustered June like a princess.

The new Fargo marriage ran at a good, swift, loving tilt, but lately Harmony had been feeling tired. "I've got everything I ever wanted," she murmured, smiling sleepily at her family and her husband.

Me, too. Thank you, Santa Claus. I won't be stuck in a motel room with Jonah this year. No Motown for me, thank goodness. Just my new sweetheart—Shep's relative—and pure country-Western, Shrimp-Elizabeth thought happily.

Jonah noted the contours of Harmony's face, her angular jaw blending into her soft mouth. She inhaled and yawned and her new lush curves lifted and shimmered over her cranberry velvet bodice. Since the first day of October, Harmony's shifting emotions had fascinated Jonah. She had explained tightly in her best methodically controlled way that she was allowing herself postbridal nerves. Wifery was a serious business—or at least, it should be. Then she threatened him with "dire consequences" if he didn't stop grinning at her. Jonah usually felt like one big grin and refused to hide his happiness. The bells jingled as he scooped her up in his arms; Harmony was shocked, to his delight. That event had taken him all day to distract her with loving, an enjoyable task. He loved seeing her flustered, warm and snugly, or her amber eyes flashing angrily at him. He just loved her.

His fingers caressed her still-flat stomach, and the tiny Fargo son nestling inside. Jonah wanted to announce to the world that Harmony carried his child, and each time he pressed his head to her womb, the baby recognized his father's voice. Keeping his thoughts off the baby was difficult, but he wanted Harmony to discover and to want his child.

Sometimes women preferred marriages without children. The thought slipped past his control.

Harmony stared at him. *Jonah Fargo. Listen, buckaroo, if I ever got pregnant with your baby, I'd fly over the moon.*

Mmm. I think we've been there a few times already.

Don't start. I'm just resting a bit, and then the mistletoe ball awaits you, Mr. Ho Ho.

"I think that I'm going to sleep all of January," Harmony said after another yawn. Pax handed her a cup of warm cider and she frowned slightly at the three cloves in the bottom of her cup. Over her head, Pax winked at Jonah.

Jonah shifted her closer, and nuzzled her unruly, beautiful hair. "Ah…Harmony, could there be other reasons that you're tired?"

She leveled a look at him. *Last night, the day before that, and the months before that? Now, would bonding and mating, real or unreal, with frequency, be a reason? To say nothing of how busy we've been and my Christmas orders,* she stated with mild irritation.

Harmony looked sharply at Pax, who had just issued a mental snicker. She looked at Jonah, her amber eyes widening. Her hand pressed his closer to her womb. *No. I would know. Women know these things right away.... Don't they?*

Don't tell me your emotions will roller coaster for the next five and a half months, Jonah drawled mentally, awed by the delight filling his wife's expression.

When? she asked.

Our wedding night. He just poured right out of me, like the love I feel for you. You were too busy at the moment, gathering him tight inside you and keeping him warm. You remember when you said that I acted dazed? When you worried about me catching cold? And kept pouring that awful rosehip tea down me?

No. It isn't possible. I would have known. Mothers always sense the baby first....

Not you. You've been busy being emotional and making love and tossing Christmas cheer everywhere. The way you wrap gifts—biting your tongue and that festival of ribbons and paper is an emotional experience in itself.... Do you want him? he asked, fearing for one heartbeat that she didn't.

You know I do. Stop preening, Jonah. Or glowing. I can see your grin under that beard.

Then Jonah nuzzled her soft cheek with his bearded one and

they shared the image of a son. "Merry Christmas, rosebud," he whispered.

"Merry Christmas to you...Daddy," she whispered back, loving Jonah, the completion of her heart, her soul.

"Ah...Santa...I think we'd better go," Janice murmured quietly and looked sharply at Pax, who was chuckling. "Don't we?" she asked archly, as she began bundling up the children against the winter weather.

"We're having a baby, aren't we, Aunt Harmony?" Jimmy asked suddenly, startling his mother.

Have to watch the little powers, Pax advised softly. *They have big antennae.*

Santa had to fly, delivering other presents, but Jonah cuddled Harmony close against him as Pax's family departed.

Snuggling back against his arms and closely gathering the shawl he had placed around her, Harmony let her hair ripple freely to the wind. "Merry Christmas, my heart," she said, her love for Jonah keeping him warm.

They listened to the wind sighing across the plains, sweeping the past away and bringing in the New Year. The time had come for peace and the future and yet, treasuring the past and dear ones.

"Merry Christmas. Come inside, rosebud. I'll keep you warm and tell you how much I love you."

It's that Santa Claus cap caper with the black nightie, isn't it? Now I know why you started thinking about that on our wedding night. Just after you seemed so stunned. You were shielding your images from me, weren't you?

Jonah grinned boyishly. *I have been very, very good.*

* * * * *

Look for

from ▼™ **SILHOUETTE**

Desire®

They're strong.
They're sexy.
They're fathers?

Three handsome heroes are in for the surprise of their lives
when they find passionate romance...and unexpected fatherhood.
Watch for these heartwarming stories celebrating love—and
parenthood—written by three delightful writers.

January 1997
GAVIN'S CHILD by Caroline Cross

February 1997
BABY FEVER by Susan Crosby

March 1997
YOU'RE WHAT! by Anne Eames

Only from Silhouette Desire

™ SILHOUETTE

Desire ®

COMING NEXT MONTH

THE COWBOY AND THE KID
Anne McAllister

Man of the Month

Taggart Jones had no intention of getting married again, but his little girl had other plans for him—and all of them involved feisty schoolteacher Felicity Albright.

FATHER ON THE BRINK
Elizabeth Bevarly

When confirmed bachelor Cooper Dugan delivered Katie Brennan's baby during a blizzard, he had no idea he was going to get a crash course in fatherhood. Then Cooper discovered parenthood was fun—and that loving Katie was even better.

GAVIN'S CHILD
Caroline Cross

Bachelors & Babies

Gavin Cantrell was stunned to return home and learn that his estranged wife Annie had given birth to his child without telling him. Now that he was back, would his dream of being a family man be fulfilled?

SILHOUETTE

Desire®

COMING NEXT MONTH

TWO WEDDINGS AND A BRIDE
Anne Eames

Brand-new bride Catherine Mason was furious when she
caught her groom kissing her bridesmaid! So she went on her
honeymoon with handsome Jake Alley—and hoped another
wedding would soon be on the way...

THE BRIDE WORE BLUE
Cindy Gerard

When Maggie Adams returned home, she never expected to
see her childhood neighbour Blue Hazzard. Could the former
gawky teenager turned hunk teach Maggie how to love again?

DONAVAN
Diana Palmer

Texan Lovers

From the moment the elegantly dressed woman walked into
the bar on the wrong side of town, rugged Texan Donavan
Langley knew she was trouble. But the lovely Fay York
awoke a tenderness in him that he'd never known...and a
desire he couldn't deny.

▼™ SILHOUETTE®

Who needs mistletoe when Santa's Little Helpers are around...

SANTA'S LITTLE HELPERS

We know you'll love this year's seasonal collection featuring three brand-new festive romances from some of Silhouette's best loved authors - including Janet Dailey

And look out for the adorable baby on the front cover!

THE HEALING TOUCH   by Janet Dailey
TWELFTH NIGHT   by Jennifer Greene
COMFORT AND JOY   by Patrica Gardner Evans

Available: December 1996   Price £4.99

SILHOUETTE

Intrigue

Angels should have wings and flowing robes - not tight black jeans and leather jackets. They should be chubby cherubs or wizened old specters - not virile and muscular and sinfully sexy.

But then again, these AVENGING ANGELS aren't your average angels!

AVENGING
ANGELS

Enter the Denver Branch of Avenging Angels and meet some of the sexiest angels this side of heaven.

Sam - THE RENEGADE by Margaret St. George
January 1997

Dashiell - THE IMPOSTOR by Cassie Miles
February 1997

and the littlest angel-to-be
Ariel - THE CHARMER by Leona Karr
March 1997

Kiel - THE SOULMATE by Carly Bishop
April 1997

They may have a problem with earthly time - but these angels have no problem with earthly pleasures!

COMING NEXT MONTH FROM

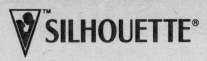

S	T	O	C	K
P	L	A	T	E

Clues:
A   To pile up
B   To ease off or a reduction
C   A dark colour
D   Empty or missing
E   A piece of wood
F   Common abbreviation for an aircraft

Please turn over for details of how to enter 🖙

How to enter...

There are two five letter words provided in the grid overleaf. The first one being STOCK the other PLATE. All you have to do is write down the words that are missing by changing just one letter at a time to form a new word and eventually change the word STOCK into PLATE. You only have eight chances but we have supplied you with clues as to what each one is. Good Luck!

When you have completed the grid don't forget to fill in your name and address in the space provided below and pop this page into an envelope (you don't even need a stamp) and post it today. Hurry—competition ends 30th June 1997.

Sihouette® Single Letter Switch
FREEPOST
Croydon
Surrey
CR9 3WZ

Are you a Reader Service Subscriber?   Yes ❑   No ❑
(I am over 18 years of age)

Ms/Mrs/Miss/Mr _____

Address _____

_____

_____ Postcode _____

One application per household.

You may be mailed with other offers from other reputable companies as a result of this application. If you would prefer not to receive such offers, please tick box.   ❑

C6L